DOCTOR JANE LANGFORD had won the respect of the tough, seasoned men of her profession in spite of her youth and feminine appeal. She was soon to join her brilliant young fiancé in a new, exciting foreign land.

Jane's future was bright with promise.

And then the blow fell. The town was rocked by a hideous crime. The leading druggist was murdered. Valuable drugs were missing. Dr. Paul Hamlin, Jane's trusted colleague, was implicated. Jane herself came under suspicion. Her reputation—even her life—was in jeopardy!

Books by Adeline McElfresh

- HILL COUNTRY NURSE
- YOUNG DOCTOR RANDALL
- DR. JANE, INTERNE
- DOCTOR JANE
- CALLING DR. JANE
- DR. JANE'S MISSION
- DR. JANE COMES HOME
- DR. JANE'S CHOICE

- Published by Bantam Books, Inc.

CALLING DR. JANE
ADELINE McELFRESH

*This low-priced Bantam Book
has been completely reset in a type face
designed for easy reading, and was printed
from new plates. It contains the complete
text of the original hard-cover edition.*
NOT ONE WORD HAS BEEN OMITTED.

CALLING DR. JANE
*A Bantam Book / published by arrangement with
Thomas Bouregy and Company*

PRINTING HISTORY
*Thomas Bouregy edition published March 1957
Bantam edition published May 1958*
*2nd printing ...... August 1958   4th printing .... May 1963
3rd printing ... November 1958   5th printing .... April 1966*

All characters and situations in CALLING DR. JANE
*are entirely fictional, and if the name of any person is
used, or if any actual happening seems portrayed, it
is coincidental.*

*All rights reserved.
© Copyright, 1957, by Adeline McElfresh.
No part of this book may be reproduced in any form,
by mimeograph or any other means, without permission in
writing. For information address: Thomas Bouregy and Company,
22 East 60th Street, New York, N. Y. 10022.*

Published simultaneously in the United States and Canada

---

*Bantam Books are published by Bantam Books, Inc., a subsidiary
of Grosset & Dunlap, Inc. Its trade-mark, consisting of the words
"Bantam Books" and the portrayal of a bantam, is registered in the
United States Patent Office and in other countries. Marca Registrada.
Bantam Books, Inc., 271 Madison Avenue, New York, N. Y. 10016.*

PRINTED IN THE UNITED STATES OF AMERICA

CALLING DOCTOR JANE

CHAPTER 1

It was cool for September and the woolly bears augured a long, hard winter, a prediction Melvina Mason did not believe. Why, the corn shucks were thin and loose as they could be and that hornet's nest she and Dr. Jane had seen out at the farm last month had been high and dry, a sure sign of mild weather all winter. Granny could count on her fingers the times she'd seen it fail, no matter what Paul Hamlin said.

Moving the rocker into the full sunshine that was forever creeping away from her, she watched the woolly little worm undulating along the white-painted porch railing. Dr. Hamlin didn't believe in woolly bears, either, that was one good thing about him, she was thinking when Sue came out, slamming the door as usual.

"Granny, darling!" Sue let out a delighted squeal. "You look exactly as though you had bitten into a persimmon!"

"A puckery one," Paul Hamlin said. "Today Mrs. Mason isn't liking me."

"Granny doesn't like any man who's in love with Jane except Bill. Do you, darling?" Sue Latham, who was Bill's sister, pecked a kiss at Granny's wrinkled cheek.

The devilish twinkle leaped from Dr. Hamlin's dark eyes to his lips. He didn't quite smile.

"Am I?"

"Of course you are. Don't bother about being gallant, Paul. I'm fully aware I'm invited to dinner simply because Jane was called out of church and goodness knows when she'll be back."

Paul gave them the smile that Sue had said the other day she'd bet made his women patients "all goose pimply." "Mrs. Mason," he said solemnly, "do you think I'll be safe with her? After all, I'm only a simple g. p."

Laughing, they went down the steps and out to the big, low-slung vanilla-ice-cream-colored convertible that Granny thought she'd like to see splashing through the mud when he got a call some midnight to come down in the river bottoms. Granny wasn't sure why she didn't like Paul Hamlin, or even if she didn't, she told herself, hitching her rocker into the sunshine that was retreating again. It was just that, sometimes, like today, he aggravated her, being as smart alecky about things a body knowed was true. Land sakes, hadn't she seen 'em prove out enough to know?

Maybe Sue was right and she didn't like Dr. Hamlin because he was in love with Dr. Jane. Or because Dr. Jane might fall in love with him. Granny wasn't sure which. Africa was an awful long ways off and if she had been in Jane Langford's shoes, she would have gone ahead and married Bill Latham and gone right along with him, the way Ed Johnson wanted her to.

Granny could hear him yet, barely whispering because that was all the strength he'd had for a long time after his heart attack. "Go along with Bill, Janie." Dr. Jane would always be Janie to the Old Doctor, Granny reckoned. "Marry the boy and go with him. I'll ask Laird to try to find someone."

"We'll find someone first." Granny could hear Dr. Jane, too. "Bill and I can be married in Africa, Dr. Ed."

Well, they had found someone, finally. Or rather, Paul Hamlin had found them. Some way or some other way, Granny wasn't sure how, he had heard there was a ready-made opportunity for a bright young doctor in Halesville and he had come.

That was two months ago and still Dr. Jane hadn't gone . . .

"She's always been the puny one, Dr. Jane. Rest of the kids big, husky, healthy as young colts, all but Cynthy, poor baby. Feeling better, darling?"

The girl, thin, with a bluish tinge to her paleness, nodded. Jane smiled at her and privately wished Mrs. Peters would keep still. Or at least not run on so in Cynthia's presence. No wonder Granny Mason said, "Myrtle Peters'll talk your arm off, give her half a chance."

"I'm glad you're feeling better, Cynthia."

The girl managed a smile.

Except that the pain was gone, she probably wasn't feeling better, Jane knew. She felt wrung out, so weak it was an effort even to smile. Hearts were like that.

"She's resting easy now, Dr. Jane. Has been ever since.

But she was bad—oh, she was bad! All gaspy and white, and—"

Dr. Jane set her black bag on the big square table beside a nearly full glass of water, a hand fan that had BARNES FUNERAL HOME printed in funereal black beneath its inexpertly copied *Ecco Homo*, and a box of Kleenex. She handed the water glass to Mrs. Peters.

"Will you get Cynthia a fresh drink, please, Mrs. Peters?" Anything to get her out of the room—

"You mustn't mind Mother, Dr. Jane," Cynthia said when her mother had gone. "She's scared."

"And worried."

Cynthia Peters nodded. "I think I almost died, Dr. Jane. I—I thought I was going to." She paused—breathless, Jane noted; then, "I couldn't breathe. There was this tightness, sort of, here." She touched her chest, and Jane nodded.

"You don't feel like that now?" she asked.

"No."

Cynthia's mother was returning, and from somewhere came voices, subdued, frightened and trying not to show it, as voices are when someone in a house is dangerously ill. Jane busied herself with the examination.

Temperature. Pulse. Listening to the telltale beat of Cynthia's heart and wishing she had the girl in the hospital at Martinsburg so that they could X-ray and do an electrocardiogram. Mrs. Peters didn't hover, and she was silent now, thank goodness for that, but she was standing board-stiff at the foot of the bed, her eyes never leaving the doctor's face as they sought any change of expression that might tell her the worst.

As she moved the stethoscope to pick up the "drip" that might be the mitral valve not functioning as it should, Jane gave her a reassuring smile.

"She's—is she going to be all right, Dr. Jane?"

"Of course she is," Dr. Jane said cheerfully.

But she might not be. Always "puny," rheumatic fever when she was seven . . .

"I'd like Dr. O'Donnell, in Martinsburg, to see her," Jane told Mrs. Peters and her husband later, when they walked to the car with her. Dr. O'Donnell was an internist, and a good one. Jane had consulted him before.

Clem Peters nodded. "Anybody you say, Dr. Jane."

"I'll ask him to meet us at the hospital."

For Cynthia was going; Jane had promised to arrange for a room and the ambulance.

She got in the car. Mustn't talk too long, Cynthia's bed was by the window, she might see them and worry—and worry she mustn't . . . "I'll see you in the morning," she promised, and drove off, waving to young Tommy, who was trudging along the lane, fishing pole on his shoulder.

The Peters farm was one of those out-of-the-way places Paul hadn't believed existed any more, miles off the ribbon of concrete that bypassed Halesville on its way to Central City. But he was learning—he was going to have to learn—that country practice was not the same as having a suite of offices in a swank Doctors' Building.

Jane frowned. She shouldn't be critical of Paul. Of course he had to get used to a small town. Even she did, and she had grown up in small towns, Halesville among them.

She slowed for a hairpin turn and then practically stopped as a small covey of quail whirred up from the grass-and-weed-grown fence row along which they had been feeding. She'd bet Paul hadn't seen many sights like that, returning from his calls in the city.

Or the broad sweep of trees and ripening corn with this narrow gravel road winding like a carelessly dropped, pale ribbon, and here and there a swatch of autumn, a red, a yellow that was like sunshine spilled all in one spot . . .

Jane smiled. Dr. Paul Hamlin, she had an idea, would hoot at such thoughts.

Halesville, sprawled in the early-afternoon sunshine that was bright on the river, appeared to be sleeping off its Sunday dinner. Not half a dozen people were astir as Jane drove along Main Street, past the grocery and the Standard station, the post office and Charley Bates's drugstore over which Clara Mae Oley, or her "relief," no doubt was catnapping at the switchboard, to the small white clapboard building that was her office and Paul's, now that Dr. Ed had given up active practice.

Inside, she called the hospital in Martinsburg, made the necessary arrangements for Cynthia Peters' admission and for Dr. O'Donnell to see the girl in the morning, and sat thinking.

How many Sunday afternoons had she spent here, at Dr. Ed's old pigeonhole desk, making out bills that, some of them, weren't paid yet and probably never would be? She had been in high school then, working Saturdays and afternoons

CALLING DOCTOR JANE

at Mr. Bates's drugstore; the forty cents an hour he'd paid her was just about all she'd had after Dad's funeral expenses were paid.

But she had managed. High school, college, medical school, working at everything from typing theses to coil winding to pay her way. Then interning at big, bustling City Hospital in Central City, and at the end of her internship joining the staff of the plush Randall Convalescent Hospital—because she had thought herself in love with Dr. MacAllen Randall's nephew Lance Hart.

After all these years of no time for love, she had fallen head over heels for Lance and for a few brief months the world was her oyster.

Hers and Lance's.

Then—

It was strange, she had often thought since. She had broken with Lance and yet it was Lance who had brought her happiness. Or rather, had driven her to it.

For he had taunted her into returning to Halesville. She would "bury" herself in "some dump" like the one she came from, he had flung at her . . .

Remembering, Jane rose. Granny couldn't keep dinner hot forever.

"Cynthia," the Old Doctor said thoughtfully. "She the string-bean blonde one?"

Dr. Jane nodded.

"Always thought she had a cardiac insufficiency of some kind. Never heard of any rheumatic fever, though . . . but if she's fourteen now, it would've been before they moved back here. Clem Peters heired the place five, six years ago."

The Old Doctor chewed his cigar for a while. "Didn't I see Paul squiring Sue off to dinner?"

"I expect you did. They had elegant steaks at the Martin House, Sue tells me." Jane laughed. " 'Elegant' being her word for them, not mine."

Dr. Johnson chuckled. Since she had come up to stay with Bill last winter, Sue Latham had become one of his favorite people.

They were sitting on the sun porch of the big, square brick house next door to the office, watching the dusk come. It was the time of day Jane liked best; there was a hush, a quietening that she found peaceful, soothing. She leaned back in the comfortably sagging wicker rocker. The spire of the little church where Bill had preached before he went to Africa, and where he would preach again when he returned, gleamed palely in the gathering darkness. Bill—

I miss you, darling—

"Eh? You say something, Janie?"

She almost had. "Not exactly."

"Now what kind of an answer is that?" The Old Doctor peered at her over his glasses. "Thought you said something or other about Bill." And after a pause, "When're you going out there, Janie?"

"Soon."

The Old Doctor didn't say anything.

Jane knew what he was thinking. She should go—she should have gone when Bill went. Dr. Ed was like Granny Mason, who made no bones about it. Jane Langford's first duty was to herself and to Bill Latham, and besides, now that Paul was here, she was free to go.

Abruptly, Jane rose.

CHAPTER 2

Dr. Jane snapped wide-awake. The telephone was ringing as only Clara Mae Oley could ring it when someone needed a doctor in the dead of night.

"Dr. Langford," Jane answered.

"Dave Payton Doctor Jane Mary says it's time!"

No commas or periods for Dave Payton now. You'd think no woman ever had been about to have a baby before, as Mary had declared laughingly when he had brought her in last week for her checkup.

"I'll meet you at the hospital, Dave."

Jane dressed quickly, in the blue flannel suit for it was chilly at this hour, ran a comb through her short dark hair, was touching lipstick to her quick-smiling mouth when Sue came.

"I thought I heard the telephone."

"They probably heard it next door." Jane laughed. "I think Clara Mae thinks I'm a heavy sleeper. It's Mary Payton's baby. I'll be at the hospital in Martinsburg, just in case. Tell Granny, will you, Sue?"

Sue nodded yawningly.

Padding barefoot along the hall, the pink chenille robe trailing regally, her hair tousled on end, she looked like a child playing at being grown up, Jane thought. She wasn't much more than a child, really. Going on twenty-one . . .

The hospital at Martinsburg was small compared to City Hospital in Central City where Jane had interned. But there the difference ended. Martinsburg Hospital had operating and delivery rooms that were as efficient and modern as anything at City, and Dr. Jane had developed a healthy respect for Dr. Laird that approached her feeling for her "Chief" at City, Dr. Warren.

Now, hurrying through the peach and frost-blue foyer, she smiled at Jenny Akers, the switchboard operator who at night doubled as admitting clerk.

"Is Mrs. Payton here yet?"

"Just." The girl laughed. "If you've never lost a father yet, you'd better look out for this one."

Jane laughed too. Poor Dave— She punched a button to bring the self-service elevator down to "1" and stood listening to the soft whirrr-rr, louder than usual in the nighttime quiet, as it descended. Behind her Jenny Akers said, "Switchboard!" to a call from within the hospital. And, "Just a minute, Doctor. I'll see."

As the elevator doors whisked open for her, Jane glanced at the Physicians' Call Board to see which other doctors were in the building. Andrews. Laird. Winters.

Apparently it was a busy night

"Good morning, Dr. Jane." Mrs. Meyer, at the nurses' station on the second floor, completed a notation on somebody's chart and hung it on the rack.

Jane said good morning and hurried along the corridor and around the corner to o. b.

"*Et tu, Brute?*" Dr. Winters, still in his whites, said as he cradled the telephone on the nurses' station worktable.

Dr. Jane smiled. She liked this big, quiet obstetrician who looked as if he would be more at home on a football field than in a delivery room. It seemed strange that Paul didn't— She set her bag on the table, peeled off her gloves. The thin, very young wail rose again.

"Yours?"

"I wouldn't doubt," Dr. Winters admitted with a grin. "He's a lusty-lunged fellow."

He went off whistling under his breath, and Dr. Jane

washed up at the lavatory in the corner before going into the labor room to see her patient.

"Hello, Mary. Dave."

Dave Payton jumped as if he'd been shot. "Dr. Jane!"

"For goodness' sake, Dr. Jane," the girl on the bed laughed, "tell him to go get a pickle with hamburger on it, or something."

But the laughter was strained and the slender fingers were clenched until white splotched her knuckles. Jane's hand closed over them reassuringly.

"Why don't you, Dave?"

"I couldn't eat a bite."

"Coffee, then?"

Dave Payton shook his head. But he went out, walking like a man in a nightmare, which in that moment, Dr. Jane knew he was.

It was going to be a perfectly normal delivery, there was nothing to be worried about, first babies are stubborn sometimes—

Dave Payton had squinched his eyes shut tight, as if the subdued light in the corridor hurt them, and now, as she went downstairs to look in on Cynthia Peters, Dr. Jane had the fleeting thought that he hadn't heard a word she had said.

She shook her head. Mary was nineteen, Dave was twenty. Younger than Sue, both of them, and already with the responsibility of a family—

Dr. Andrews' light was off when she went through the foyer but Dr. Laird's and Dr. Winters' still were on. Jane paused at the receptionist's desk.

"What goes on?" she asked, indicating the call board.

Freckles marched merrily across Jenny's nose when she wrinkled it. "Confab. Dr. Laird is wearing that 'great-stone-face' look of his."

"At this hour? Gracious."

"I know." The girl sobered. "I think it has something to do with that emergency that came in around midnight. Miss Delman called Dr. Andrews and pretty soon he called Dr. Laird on the double. They've been huddling ever since they came out of Surgery. Dr. Andrews just left."

"Well," Jane said, and after a minute went on down the corridor.

CALLING DOCTOR JANE

An oxygen tank and tent stood outside Cynthia's door. Ready if they needed it, but thank goodness they hadn't.

"Good morning, Miss Lancaster."

The short, red-haired nurse was tiptoeing to reach the top shelf of the drug cabinet, and three or four of the tiny paper cups in which pills were taken to patients were lined up on the cabinet.

She turned, smiling. "Whew. Being short and dumpy may have its compensations but I don't know what they are. O. b.?"

Dr. Jane nodded and watched the nurse consult an order, drop a tiny white pill into a cup and set it on the note bearing a physician's instructions and the patient's name and room number.

"Is Cynthia Peters having a good night?"

"Not too. She's restless."

"Is she awake now?"

"She was when I looked in a few minutes ago."

More pills, two large pink ones this time. When Dr. Jane went along the hall toward Cynthia's room, Miss Lancaster was stretching to return the bottles to their high perch.

Jane stood for a moment outside Cynthia's door, listening to the not-quite utter stillness that was the hospital at night. Somewhere nearby a patient snored whistlingly. Miss Lancaster's crepe soles whispered to the cork-tiled floor as she passed with her tray of medications. From inside the room came the rustle of sheets.

Dr. Jane stepped inside. "Awake, Cynthia?"

"Yes, Dr. Jane."

It was a tremulous whisper. For all her brave front in front of her family, Cynthia was a little girl now, frightened. Jane squeezed her hand.

"Mary Payton is upstairs to have her baby," she explained, so Cynthia wouldn't add two and two and get sixteen, "and I ran down for a minute. How are you feeling?"

"Better, I guess."

"Good."

Her fingers sought the girl's pulse. Was it stronger than it had been yesterday? She was breathing free and easy now. "I'm going to ask Miss Lancaster to make you some hot cocoa to help you sleep, Cynthia. Would you like that?"

"Yes." A pause; then, "Will you be here when the other—when Dr. O'Donnell comes?"

"Before he comes," Jane promised.

Dr. Jane drove home in the mother-of-pearl, mauve-and-pink dawn. This was starting out to be one of those days, she thought, not even bothering to hide the yawn. She would snatch two or three hours' sleep, then drive back to the hospital to consult with Dr. O'Donnell about Cynthia Peters and to see her other hospital patients. In the afternoon she would keep office hours in Stewart, a village not far from Halesville, in which she and Dr. Ed had opened an office for two afternoons a week just before the Old Doctor's heart attack . . .

"It's an experiment and we may not earn our salt," the Old Doctor had said, and sometimes, at first, Jane had thought he was right. The small waiting room had remained distressingly empty, or very nearly so.

It still wasn't crowded. But it seldom was empty for long—and Paul was wrong, she thought now. Time spent there wasn't wasted.

Frowning, Dr. Jane let the car coast to a silent stop in front of the sprawling old house she had rented cattycornered from Dr. Ed Johnson's big, square brick house and its adjoining rose garden and the white clapboard building with clerestory windows that wooed light into the offices even on the drabbest day.

Not even Paul could criticize the examining rooms and the small, simply equipped operating room in which tonsilectomies and other minor surgery not requiring hospitalization frequently were performed. Dr. Jane sat for moments looking at the clinic and, when a flicker of movement caught the corner of her eye, at the Old Doctor's house.

A very early bird? Or was Dr. Ed aprowl, worrying how things had gone?

Bless his heart, Jane thought warmly. He had delivered both Dave and Mary, as well as Mary's mother, and she knew what it would have meant to him to have been able to deliver Dave's and Mary's baby . . .

Her lashes feeling strangely damp, she hurried into the house.

Dr. O'Donnell waved his sandwich to get her attention and Dr. Jane threaded her way through the crowded small restaurant across the street from the hospital to the table where he sat with Dr. Jancieski, the radiologist.

"O'Donnell on etiquette," Jancieski jeered friendlily. "Hi, Jane."

CALLING DOCTOR JANE 11

Smiling a hello, Jane pulled out a chair and sat down.

"I just looked at those X-rays, Jane," Dr. O'Donnell began, and stopped when the waitress came.

"Ham on rye and a glass of milk," Jane told her.

The internist continued, "There's enlargement, all right." He shook his head. "Kid like that—"

He let it go, and after a pause said, "I'd like to do some more tests before I say mitral stenosis."

Dr. Jane nodded, and O'Donnell concentrated frowningly on his sandwich.

Scar tissue from that rheumatic fever inflammation, keeping the mitral valve from closing. Blood flowing back into the auricle every time the ventricle contracted, the heart straining and trying hard, and enlarging— Absently, Jane bit into her own sandwich.

After a time, Dr. Jancieski rose, said "See you two," and left. Dr. O'Donnell brought out the old briar about which he got kidded unmercifully at nearly every medical society meeting and tamped into it what Dr. Winters solemnly declared was "long green."

"Ready?" he asked as he lit up. "I'd like you to look at those X-rays."

Jane nodded.

They walked back to the hospital in sunshine that was only pleasantly warm although it was noon, and Jane thought that Granny's weather prophets might be right about a mild winter but it was going to be an early fall. She watched a maple leaf, prematurely red, flutter down, and soon there would be flying wedges of geese headed south.

When you saw them, Granny said, you could look out . . . Jane smiled to herself and a boy crossing the hospital foyer on crutches grinned back.

"Doin' all right, ain't I, Doc?"

"You're doing fine."

"One of your patients?" Dr. O'Donnell asked when they were out of earshot.

"No. I think he's Dr. Andrews'."

X-ray was down the corridor that led to the ambulance entrance and the emergency room, where last night a patient had been brought in who had upset Dr. Laird, Jane remembered and wondered if that had been Dr. Laird summoning Dr. Winters when she had arrived in o. b.

"Here you are, Dr. O'Donnell," the X-ray technician was

saying, and the internist handed the eight-by-ten films to Jane.

The beginnings of a frown plucked at her brows as she studied them.

Later, when she had a few minutes between patients at the office in Stewart, she recalled the X-rays from what Paul would call the "Cynthia Peters' pigeonhole" of her mind. Bone structure, that enlarged heart, every light and shadow crystal-clear in her memory, she sat thinking about them, and about the electrocardiographic tracings of Cynthia's heart, until footsteps in the waiting room announced a patient.

Dr. Jane rose.

"Good afternoon," she greeted the woman and small boy who were standing uncertainly in the middle of the room.

"You the lady doctor?"

"Yes."

Jane smiled at the little boy, who was pulling back. Obviously it was he who was to be her patient, and a reluctant one.

"Well, he run a thorn in his leg and it ain't lookin' right." The woman tugged the boy around in front of her. "Now you behave, Sammie!"

It certainly wasn't "lookin' right," Jane saw when the child was on her examining table *sans* jeans. The flesh around the ugly, festering sore on his thigh was hard and feverish.

"We thought it'd be all right, Sam and me," the woman said. She wet her lips worriedly when Jane began to get her instruments.

Sammie watched, suspicion and fright in his wide, brown-velvet eyes. Jane smiled at him.

"You're not going to like this, Sammie, but you're going to be a big boy, aren't you?"

Hesitantly, and after a longish moment of mind-making-up, he nodded.

"It was a mean ol' thorn."

Jane agreed that it was.

A local anesthetic . . . a quick incision and drainage . . . the bandage that Jane let Sammie "help" put on. Penicillin . . .

"There you are, Sammie! I guess we showed that mean old thorn, didn't we?"

Grinning shyly, Sammie slid off the table.

After they had gone, Jane sterilized her instruments and

cleaned up. It would be nice to have an office nurse; perhaps one day they would have, at least at the office in Halesville. Paul said they were medieval not to have one, as well as a secretary. Who ever heard of the town switchboard operator keeping track of a doctor's calls?

Remembering, Jane shut the white cabinet in which she kept nstruments, bandages, and medications with a sharp little click.

For a time the afternoon was as afternoons usually were in Stewart. Leisurely. With nothing more serious than Joel Henry's hay fever which would hang on until frost "consarn it!" and Sibbie Neidlinger's aching "j'ints."

Then, "Joe's caught in the cornpicker, Doctor!" a woman screamed into the telephone. "Joe Hiram! His whole arm, almost!"

"I'll be right there!"

Jane hung up. "I'm sorry, Mrs. Neidlinger. There has been a cornpicker accident. I'll stop by your house when I—"

"For lord's sake! Who?"

Jane told her.

Hastily she checked her bag, got bandages and surgical instruments from the cabinet so that she would be ready for anything, and ran out to the car. Mrs. Neidlinger stood in the door, watching.

The Hiram farm was three or four miles out of Stewart. Jane drove as she seldom did, the accelerator to the floorboards most of the way. A man could bleed to death so quickly . . .

After forever, it seemed, she was there, and climbing into somebody's Jeep to go tearing along a rutted farm road to Joe Hiram's back forty.

"I put a tourniquet on when I found 'im!" the lean, raw-boned driver shouted into the wind that was pummeling them. "But I don't know. He was working by himself when it happened. Hang on, Doc!"

Jane hung on for dear life as they careened around a bend and across a plank bridge with no guard rails.

Up ahead, men clustered around the cornpicker broke rank and when the Jeep stood on its nose in a skidding, dust-raising stop there were eager hands to take her bag, to hand her down.

"He's still conscious," one of the men volunteered.

Then silence, the profound silence that, somehow, is fear and dread and hope and prayer all at once. Even the wind hushed its questing through the corn and the lone crow flying lumberingly overhead was still.

"Here's the doctor, Joe."

The woman who was holding Joe Hiram's other hand gave it a squeeze and moved away. From the far side of the field the crow cawed, the sound harsh and strident, as if he were angry with the man for breaking the spell.

"Doc—"

Cords in Joe Hiram's neck stood out, the muscle knotted hard in his jaw worked.

"Doc," he began again, "I don't care how much it hurts, but—save my arm, will you?"

Dr. Laird was waiting and in minutes Jane was scrubbed up and in surgical gown and mask, with her short dark hair secured in a snug surgical cap, ready to assist.

She looked at the horribly mangled arm and Joe Hiram's plea haunted her again. "*I don't care how much it hurts, but—save my arm, will you?*"

Could Dr. Laird?

With an arm as *shredded* as that one, could *anyone*?

Please, God—

CHAPTER 3

Pesky mosquito . . . Bill Latham—the Reverend Mr. William F. Latham, late of Halesville, Indiana, U.S.A.—swung a hefty swat in the general direction of the annoying buzzzz-zz, which went right on buzz-buzz-buzzing around his ear.

"Persistent things, aren't they?" Al Rodarmel, whom Bill described in his letters home as a circuit-riding missionary doctor, said.

"They are that."

They walked on through pools of sun and shadow, along the sluggish stream that, off yonder somewhere, emptied into the Congo.

"Look at the devils." Dr. Rodarmel gestured. "Millions of them."

There probably were. And tsetse flies. And, Bill Latham thought, the Lord and botanists knew what else off there in the jungle through which the natives came and went at will although he didn't see how they could do it and stay alive.

Bill swatted again and was rewarded with blessed silence, even if only for the time.

"Get him?"

"I think so."

"Someday—" the doctor began and stopped, words and gaze lost somewhere in the sea of sunshine ahead, where the jungle ended abruptly in a natural clearing in which huddled the handful of thatched buildings that was the mission station.

Bill didn't say anything. He knew the doctor's dream: an Africa free of disease, and of the prejudices that were worse than disease.

They talked of it, sometimes, when the doctor made his regular visits to the mission outpost and the tropical night was velvety beyond the circle of light from the gasoline lamp. The new Africa, not a Utopia, for they were practical men—

Al Donaldson was like Jane, Bill Latham thought. Dedicated. He touched the pocket into which he had slipped her letter, which Al had brought out in the mail packet.

Just a note, dashed off between Mr. Christy's blood pressure and Jimmie Cleves' cold so that Mr. Christy could take it back to the post office with him. She and Granny and Sue were fine. The Old Doctor was behaving—

Realizing he had taken the letter out, he shoved it back into his pocket. It wasn't the briefness that bothered him— he was used to Jane's hastily scribbled notes—but something was there, between the lines. The same something that had been in all of her letters lately . . .

Dr. Laird was a man inspired, Jane Langford thought with the strangely detached part of her mind that was not attuned to the surgeon's and if Joe Hiram had a useful arm when this was over, it would be because of him. Deftly she tied off a bleeder. Miss Bartlett, one of the surgical nurses, swabbed.

The hiss of the sterilizer . . . Dr. Laird's terse order or a request for an instrument . . . the anesthetist's quiet "Respiration normal" that was music to their ears.

Snip away a shred of hopelessly damaged tissue . . . cut —clamp—probe for a severed tendon. How long had the operation been going on? Joe Hiram's shattered radius had been rebuilt, sliver by sliver, almost; the carpals and metacarpals had been reconstructed—

"Cornpickers," Dr. Laird said in the same tone he would have said "Suture!" or "Hemostat!" "When will men learn?"

Dr. Jane knew how he felt. A few seconds to shut off the machine and Joe Hiram wouldn't be here; he wouldn't have lost those fingers . . .

A nurse blotted beads of sweat from the surgeon's forehead; his long, slender, sensitive hands didn't falter in their task. Another tendon "one" again. Probe—sew—now remove a clamp. To Joe Hiram's wife, the waiting would seem an eternity. . . .

It was over, finally. Joe Hiram would have his arm—but would he ever use it? In the small restaurant across from the hospital, Jane sat looking into her empty cup as if the answer were there, thinking, seeing again Dr. Laird in that moment when the operation was finished—straightening, flexing his shoulders that must have been aching with weariness.

What had he been thinking in that long moment when he stood looking down at his patient, at the right arm swathed in white and immobilized, at the craggy, unhandsome face into which a bit of color was beginning to return?

"More coffee, Dr. Jane?" the waitress asked.

"Not this time, Donna."

Donna nodded. These doctors. Come in at all hours and bolt a sandwich or order coffee and let it get cold while they talked about somebody's insides. Or thought about them. And all the time telling their patients to eat regular meals, too.

"Yes, sir?" She stopped at a table where a man had just sat down.

"Black coffee."

"Anything to eat, sir?"

"Hamburger—anything," the man said, in a voice as haggard and drawn as his face.

They got them that way, Donna was thinking as she said, "Yes, sir." Being right across from the hospital they sure got all kinds.

Dr. Jane rose, fumbled in a pocket of the blue flannel suit for change. If she could go home now and let a good hot tub relax her—but she couldn't. She had to look in on Joe

CALLING DOCTOR JANE

Hiram again, and she had promised Mrs. Neidlinger she would stop by.

And then there was Mary Payton and the baby—and Cynthia Peters.

Visiting hours were over and the hospital was settling down for the night, although it hadn't, yet. As Jane went along the corridor toward Joe Hiram's room, there were low voices, a cough, the pad of slippers as some ambulatory patient put off going to bed. In one of the rooms a woman was sobbing softly. Into her pillow, Jane thought compassionately.

Post-operative, probably, and kitten-weak. Or she was going to Surgery in the morning and was frightened—

She paused outside Joe Hiram's door. Back along the hall a nurse came out of a room, left the door carefully ajar, and disappeared into the room next door. The one in which the woman was crying, Jane hoped.

She stepped inside. "Well, Mrs. Hiram?"

"He's coming out of it, I think, Dr. Langford. Sometimes he mumbles and—and struggles." Her voice caught, and Jane nodded. He was doing it now.

Mumbling, half-emerging from anesthesia, fighting to stay "up" and losing. Jane knew. She touched a quiet hand to his forehead, found the pulse in his good wrist.

"Have you eaten?"

Mrs. Hiram shook her head.

"There's a restaurant across the street."

The blue eyes seemed undecided. "If he should regain consciousness while I'm gone—"

"I'll be here. I want to check his blood pressure and temperature, anyway."

"Well-l-l—"

With a worried glance at her husband, who was lying quietly now, Mrs. Hiram said, "All right. I am hungry."

After she had gone, Dr. Jane took Joe Hiram's temperature, listened to the steady beat of his heart. The man must have the constitution of a Missouri mule.

An uneasy moan rose to his lips. "Clar—" The word—was his wife's name Clara? Jane wondered—went trailing off; his good arm thrashed the bed.

"Easy, Mr. Hiram." Jane put a firm hand on his arm.

"Do you need me, Doctor?"

"I think not, Miss Beckett. Thank you."

With a nod and a smile, the nurse went out.

Joe Hiram wet his lips, the tip of his tongue exploring them cautiously. His Adam's apple bobbed, a muscle in his jaw twitched. For a long minute he lay perfectly still.

Then his good hand crept, fearful, dreadfilled, across his sheet-covered body—

"Well, if you ask me"—the orderly shifted his weight to the other hip and went on leaning—"somebody's going to catch hail Columbia!"

"Broth-er, are they!" Jenny Akers agreed fervently. "You should have seen Doc Laird last—Oh, hello, Dr. Jane."

The orderly undraped from Jenny's desk in a hurry. "Leaving us, Doctor?"

"I think it's about time, don't you? Any calls, Jenny?"

Jenny shook her head.

"Good. I'm so tired I'm numb."

She was, Jane realized as she walked down the block to where Joe Hiram's neighbor had parked her car . . . Flimsy clouds were racing across the moon and there was a new chill to the wind that was rustling the leaves.

". . . . somebody's going to catch hail Columbia!"

So Guy Cowling should have seen Dr. Laird last night, should he? "*Confab*," Jenny had said then. "*Dr. Laird is wearing that 'great-stone face' look of his.*"

Getting in her car, Jane sat for minutes, letting the weariness wash over her in waves. She could see Mrs. Neidlinger in the morning—

Thinking that, she touched the starter button.

But when she reached the Y she took the arm of the road that led to Stewart . . .

Rain was pelting spitefully against the window when Jane awoke. A cold, misery-making rain that would make Mrs. Neidlinger's "j'ints" ache worse than ever. Jane got out of bed, pulled on her tailored navy flannel robe, and went quietly downstairs.

She loved this old house, with its huge rooms and high ceilings. Her room and Sue's, both of them large, square, many-windowed, were upstairs; Granny's bedroom, a "spare" bedroom, the living room, dining room, kitchen, even a "parlor" were down. And across the breezeway that probably had been called a dogtrot when the house was built were a smokehouse, a washhouse, a "summer kitchen."

The "parlor" would be right for Bill's study, handy to the front door when members of his congregation came calling. But Bill was enchanted with the summer kitchen—

As she put on the coffee, Jane smiled at the memory. They had been "house shopping," as Bill put it, in the spring, when they had expected to be married after church one Sunday, take a few days' honeymoon and be back in time for Bill to preach the next Sunday. Before she had even heard of a missionary named Barker Caldwell . . .

"Sa-a-ay! This is all right!" Bill's voice came from somewhere out back, Jane wasn't sure where, there was so much room in this sprawling old house. "Jane, come look!"

Jane touched the newel post again, just to be sure it was as satin-soft as she remembered from the first caress. Walnut, Mr. Bates said it was. Almost the whole house was walnut, dating from the pioneer days when walnut trees spread over acres of this part of the country. "I'm coming!" she called.

Oh, it was lovely! Dark, gleaming floors, shining walnut dado in the dining room, that old hanging lamp, this funny little dogtrot— She paused, visualizing wicker chairs and a table with maybe one of her medical journals and Bill's typewriter.

"Jane—"

Bill emerged, slightly spider-webby, from one of the three small, peak-roofed buildings that stood elbow to elbow beyond the dogtrot. "Honey, you ought to see in that loft!"

"You have, I see," she laughed.

"You and Granny and Sue can have the rest of it, but this"—gesturing—"is mine."

"Cobwebs and all?"

The grin touched his warm gray eyes first, then sprang to one corner of his mouth. Bill's smiles were like that.

"Cobwebs, squeaking hinges and all. Listen." He swung the door shut, and *creeeakkk!* Jane shuddered. "But I'll fix that."

The spick-and-spanness of the house didn't extend to out here. Long unused, the random-width boards in the floor were carpeted by decades of dust. Webs festooned windows and rafters, and Bill's footprints were relatively clean patches on the narrow stairway to the loft, which like the first floor obviously had been the dumping ground of generations.

"I'll sort all this stuff and clean it up—"

"Which first?"

"Dr. Langford, if you're laughing at me—" As he drew

her to him, Jane could feel herself drowning in his eyes . . .

And the next week Barker Caldwell had come to lecture in Martinsburg.

Jane leaned her forehead against the window and watched tiny runnels of water go chasing each other down the pane. It was a wonderful opportunity for Bill, the chance of a lifetime, really. Not every young preacher, let alone one in a town the size of Halesville, got invited to be one of Barker Caldwell's right hands.

But—

Abruptly she turned from the window. The coffee was perking.

"Why not dinner?" Paul challenged.

Dr. Jane shook her head. "Don't be argumentative."

"You're the one who said no."

Jane smiled. "I'm sorry, Paul. I'm tired, and the rain depresses me, I guess."

The clouds had broken briefly during the afternoon, but it had been raining again for the last hour, a misty drizzle that hung a pearl-toned halo around the street lights.

"You still have to eat," Paul reminded her.

He shrugged into his topcoat, took her navy cashmere from the hatrack in the corner. "Hurry up before somebody has a gall bladder."

Laughing, Jane rose. Somebody would, just about the time they got to coffee. Or if not a gall bladder, a sniffle. They were of equal importance to the person who had them.

"I'll have to change," she said as she slipped into the coat.

"Right. Half an hour?"

"Three quarters. I've a feeling I'm going to be poky."

Shaking his head, Paul said, "Not a second longer than forty-four minutes."

After he had gone, Jane went through the building turning off lights, turning down the thermostat, closing a window against the damp chill. Beyond the window Dr. Ed's rose garden was sodden in the thickening dusk. How long it seemed, this evening, since there had been a riot of color and fragrance out there.

In another mood the mist would be enchanting, she thought as she drove the block home. She used to love walking in the rain. Bill did. He always said he could work out a knotty problem walking in the rain, or the snow. He was closer to God, he guessed, because the rain or the snow, or the sunshine in the fields, sheared away the unimportant things.

Bill—

The mist was like a remembered kiss against her face, cool, gentle, and as she walked toward the house the elm tree weepingly dropped a handful of leaves.

"Granny," Jane called toward the kitchen, "Paul is taking me to supper. I hope that isn't chicken I smell."

"And dressin'." Granny opened the oven to peer. "It'll keep, I reckon."

The old darling, trying so hard to hide her displeasure and it stuck out all over her. Jane gave her an impulsive hug. "I'm sorry, Granny. I didn't have time to warn you. He just asked me."

"Who asked you what?" Sue demanded from halfway down the basement steps.

"Paul. To go to supper."

A flutter of footsteps deposited Sue in the kitchen. "Well, it's about time!"

Jane laughed. "Gracious, Sue, Paul has taken me out before."

"Sure, but you've never been all adither about it before. You are, too," she said as a protest sprang to Jane's lips. "Your eyes are all lit up with that inner happiness Bill is always talking about, and if an invitation to supper can do that to you—"

The trouble was, it could. It *had*. But Sue was wrong. She hadn't been in a cocoon ever since Bill left; she had been busy, too busy, perhaps—

"Boo!" Paul Hamlin said softly, and Jane smiled.

"I'm sorry. I was thinking."

"It's a bad habit." The dark eyes caressed her.

"So I've been told."

Somewhere nearby the gypsy girl struck a plaintive chord on her guitar and the sound sent an anticipatory shiver up Jane's spine. This was music such as she had never heard before, wild, untamed, and yet touchingly tender. Now the girl was moving through the dining room again, slowly, sometimes pausing beside a table, plucking from the strings notes that were rich and ripe and full of yearnings, or singing a song that was hauntingly lovely even when you didn't understand the words.

Across the room the club's manager appeared in the doorway, his eyes searching among the diners, and until he skirted the room toward Dr. Winters, Jane held her breath.

"Oh, oh," Paul said. "Winters just got tagged."

Jane nodded.

The girl was coming toward their table now, moving with an infinite grace, singing her love song only to the person into whose eyes she was looking in that brief span before her luminous dark eyes, her song, moved on. Suddenly Jane felt trapped. She wasn't Jane Langford, M. D., a busy general practitioner. She was Jane Langford, woman, and if that girl sang to her, all the defenses her professional reserve had built up would go crumbling.

"Let's go, Paul."

He stared at her. "Now? But we haven't finished."

"Please, Paul. I—I just remembered something."

CHAPTER 4

Boxtown, that part of Halesville that lay downriver, where Clay Morton's factory lorded it over the rows of neat, small houses, was astir early, as usual. The shifts changed at seven; at five till- a whistle reminded the lagging, and for ten minutes before and fifteen minutes after the whistle blast you would have thought this was Central City and not tiny Halesville.

Almost at the factory gates, Dr. Jane signaled and awaited her chance to turn left. No wonder Mrs. Woods' asthma was worse this morning. Look at that smoke—

She sighed. She knew what Clay Morton would say, he had said it often enough: most of the time it was all right, but when the atmosphere was heavy, as it was this morning, could he help it if the smoke went right down to the ground?

In a way he was right, Jane thought, slipping through a gap in the line of homeward-bound workers.

But it was his factory and his smoke, and the people most affected were the families of men who worked in his factory.

She parked in front of a house that was a carbon copy of every other house in the block.

A man in overalls answered her knock. "Come in, Dr. Jane. Ma's in here."

He led the way to a front bedroom, where Mrs. Woods, wrinkled and worn out by spasmodic coughing, was propped up in bed.

"Dr. Jane," she wheezed, "I—"

Another seizure interrupted her.

"It's that infernal smoke," her son said, and Jane, her lips pressed tight in Granny's green-persimmon pucker, nodded. If Clay Morton could see this old woman gasping, struggling, fighting for breath—

But Clay Morton wouldn't see. He had rebuilt Boxtown after that tornado slashed through it last year, had taken his bow on the newspapers, and then he had climbed right back on the pedestal from which he surveyed his world . . .

The epinephrin was taking effect now, the paroxysm was passing. Jane patted the blue-veined hand clutching the sun-burst quilt. It was too much to hope for that Clay Morton should have stayed changed, she thought. He had been a selfish, tight-fisted old skinflint the day he was born.

"Jim"—Mrs. Woods' voice was thin, weak—"you go on to work."

"I'll punch in late, Ma." He didn't tell her it already was "late." "It'll be all right."

The old woman blew her nose and wiped her eyes.

Outside a few minutes later, Jim Woods said worriedly, "She can't stand much more of that, Dr. Jane. I've been thinking—"

He hesitated. For a long moment he stood looking at the factory, its tall stacks belching smoke that this morning mushroomed and then hung like a pall over Boxtown.

"I've been thinking," he repeated. "If I can get a little place in the country—would it help Ma?"

"Yes."

"Just smell it, Dr. Jane! No wonder Ma can't breathe; it's a wonder any of us can."

It was, but younger, stronger lungs than Mrs. Woods' managed to sift enough oxygen from the polluted air. They would go on managing to—for a while. Then it would be too late.

"Be sure to fill that prescription this afternoon, Mr. Woods. I left some capsules for now."

She left him standing there on the cramped little stoop—

but only in the flesh. Memory of the lined face and its worry, and of the old woman's misery, followed her on house calls and to the hospital in Martinsburg, and back to afternoon office hours. She had to try again.

But what?

This time—what?

"I don't know, Janie." Mr. Bates wagged his head when she mentioned it that evening. "I read in the papers about smoke control, but it's always in some big city like Louisville or Pittsburgh."

"Or Los Angeles," Sam Christy, who had stopped in the drugstore for a cup of coffee to see him home, volunteered. "Out there they're always talkin' inversion. Someday it's goin' to happen."

Mr. Bates drew Jane's Coke. "Here, though—" He hesitated. "I don't know."

"Don't worry, Doc. It'll clear up tomorrow."

"Or the wind will change. I know."

Jane's smile was bleak. How many times had she heard that, or words that said the same ineffectual thing?

They probably thought she was tilting at a windmill. Halesville was small, with only one factory although it was a large one, and had air pollution only infrequently.

And, she couldn't help thinking, Clay Morton was a big man in this town—

Jane Langford! she scolded herself.

It wasn't fair to accuse Mr. Bates or Mr. Christy of knuckling under. They weren't. They just didn't see.

She finished her Coke and slid off the stool.

"Jim Woods was in for his mother's epinephrin," the druggist said. "Said something about a place in the country. That ought to help."

"They can't all move out, Mr. Bates."

"Now, Janie—"

Sam Christy chuckled. "Let her go, Charley. Clay Morton needs a thorn in his side."

She was that, all right, Jane thought as she went out to the car.

But being a thorn wasn't enough, and she already had tried reasoning, pleading, even threatening, and what did Clay Morton do?

"Good Lord, Dr. Langford! I rebuilt Boxtown. Do you want me to air-condition it, too?"

That had been one time.

Another: "*Now just a minute, Dr. Jane.*" Let's-be-reasonable fairly dripped from his voice. "*Let's be reasonable—*"

Jane could have shaken him. Perhaps she should have, Tom Winters had said when she brought the matter up at medical society meeting.

Sam Christy was right. The sky cleared in the night, and next morning smoke spiraled high above the factory and swept briskly southward, trailing long, thinning plumes.

But next week or next month—and what of Mrs. Woods and those others with respiratory ailments *then?*

Vaguely uneasy, because there must be something she could do and she wasn't doing it, she checked her medical bag and left the office on morning calls before Paul came down. Eight o'clock in the morning was a weird, in-between hour to Paul, who frankly admitted that he had no idea country doctors got out and around so early.

Jane frowned at the sunlit panorama unfolding in front of her. She wished Paul wouldn't say things like that, no matter if he did think them. It was so easy for people to misunderstand.

And being understood now, while he was new to Halesville, was important to him . . .

After half a dozen calls, in town and out, and at the last house checking with Clara Mae Oley to see if there had been any more calls for her, Jane was driving toward Martinsburg. Dr. O'Donnell wanted to see her about Cynthia Peters, about whom he had been consulting a specialist in Central City. And Mary Payton wanted to go home today—

She found Dr. O'Donnell in the lab where he and the pathologist, Dr. Sears, were huddling over somebody's platelets.

"Be with you in a jiffy, Jane," Dr. O'Donnell said. "Then, Lee, you'd say—"

Jane listened and didn't listen—she heard the words but they were water off a duck's back. Suppose Dr. Rinderle, who was the heart man in Central City, had decided Cynthia was inoperable?

How could she tell Cynthia when, for the first time the child could remember, there was hope?

A technician was doing a blood sedimentation. Another, who was recording the results of a test she had just finished, stopped to answer the telephone.

"For you, Dr. Sears."

The pathologist nodded and went on machine-gunning words at Dr. O'Donnell as he crossed to take the instrument from her. "Sears!" he barked into it.

He listened.

Dr. O'Donnell studied the toes of his shoes, frowningly, as if he didn't quite like what he saw there, Jane thought. Obviously he had forgotten her. But in a few minutes, when they would be discussing Cynthia, he would be just as oblivious to everything, and everyone, else . . .

A few minutes later he was. The suspected purpura had been filed away in his mind, to be summoned again at a time when it would have his undivided attention.

Now it was Cynthia's mitral stenosis that gripped him; there were no halfway measures with Dr. Michael O'Donnell, which, the Old Doctor said, was one of the things that made him the doctor he was.

Jane listened while he recounted his telephone consultation with the Central City specialist. It was one of several during which the two men had discussed Dr. O'Donnell's and Jane's diagnoses, the results of specific tests done at Dr. Rinderle's request, and Cynthia's entire medical history.

"He wants to see her a week from Tuesday, Jane," Dr. O'Donnell summed up as they arrived at the door of the medical records library. Jane had an idea his patient's purpura was nudging him again. "He's already made arrangements for her to check in at City . . . Isn't that your old stamping ground?"

Jane nodded.

City . . . riding the ambulances, taking her turn in the free clinic on Thursdays, making her rounds through seemingly endless corridors.

"Sometimes it seems forever ago," she said.

"I know." O'Donnell's smile was reminiscent of his own internship. "And sometimes only yesterday."

Jane nodded.

The internist scrubbed his chin with a loose fist. "I told him you'd call him, Jane. After you've talked to the girl's family."

"Dr. Andrews," the intercom began intoning. "Dr. Andrews, call the switchboard, please. Doc—"

"I suppose you've heard about Andrews' hot potato," Dr. O'Donnell said.

"Yes and no. A little."

"And about three different versions, probably none of them the right one, the way Andrews and Laird have clammed up."

"And Tom," Jane said.

"Winters? Well." Bony knuckles massaged his chin again. "Well, well."

Version number four, Jane thought as she went downstairs. Or at least, another tangent. She wondered what were the "three different versions" Dr. O'Donnell had heard, or if that had been merely a figure of speech corralling the rumors.

About the only thing on which they agreed was the woman in three-fourteen, along the corridor from Joe Hiram's room. The woman she had heard sobbing the other night.

"Dr. Jancieski," the intercom began again, "Dr. Jancieski—"

"Good morning, Cynthia."

Cynthia Peters smiled a good morning. "I was waiting for you. Miss Bailey said you were in the hospital. What did he say?"

"You're going to Central City next week."

"Is he going to operate then?"

Not a flicker of fear. Or of doubt. Jane's heart twisted. "I don't know exactly, Cynthia."

Cynthia's blue eyes were steady. "You mean he might decide—not to?"

The hospital sounds around them, even the hospital, the warm, soft blue of the walls of Cynthia's room and the handful of bittersweet that Tommy had brought her, suddenly ceased to exist for either of them.

"Cynthia—"

Jane sat on the bed. The owl-solemn eyes didn't waver, but a tremble stirred the girl's lips.

"We think he will, Cynthia," Jane said gently. "Dr. O'Donnell and I. But we won't know for sure until Dr. Rinderle sees you. He probably will do over again all the tests we have done here, and very likely will do some more." She smiled encouragingly. "He may send you home to rest a while—"

Almost shyly, Cynthia touched her hand. "It's all right, Dr. Jane. I—it's just that I want so m-much to be well again."

Jane could have howled, she told Granny as they lingered at the supper table that night.

"Myrtle Peters will, I expect, when you tell her."

Jane shook her head. "I don't think so. There's something about trouble that strengthens a person." She broke a carrot stick. "I told Cynthia to tell them I'd drive out tonight. Why don't you come along for the ride?"

"There's class meetin'—"

Which Granny wouldn't miss for the world, Jane knew. You never could tell what juicy morsel Lucy Gray might come up with . . .

She smiled to herself. Class "meetin'," Ladies' Aid, that frayed spot in the church carpet—in her own mind Granny still was Bill's housekeeper and there were things she had to look out for.

"How do I look?"

Sue, wearing a pale-blue swatch of summer sky that made her magnolia skin with its spatter of freckles creamier than ever, pirouetted into the room.

"Think Paul will like me? Jane, may I wear your wrap?"

"You may. This must be quite a date."

"Oh, it is!" Sue stood on one foot to inspect the slim heel of a sandal. "This piano duo is out of this world, Paul says. Are my seams straight?"

"As a die."

Sue reached for a carrot stick, began nibbling it. "We're going to the Country Club afterwards. Clay and Lola Morton are giving a supper. Wouldn't you know Paul would latch onto them? Ohhhh, there he is now!" she said breathlessly, as the brass knocker sounded.

She was off, hummingbird-swift, and a moment later Paul's baritone was rolling through the house.

"Stand still, sweetheart, let me look at you—" punctuated by an appreciative whistle.

Not looking at Granny, Jane rose and went into the hall.

"Isn't she stunning, Paul?"

"That makes two of you."

Sue's laugh tinkled happily. "If I didn't know about Bill, I think I'd be jealous. I'll be right down, Paul," she called as she ran up the stairs.

"I do know about Bill and I am jealous."

Jane didn't look at him, and then she did, because she couldn't help it, as if some force in those dark eyes impelled her to. He wasn't quite smiling, then even the trace of laughter went and Jane's breath caught in her throat.

"Jane—"

"Here I come, ready or not!" Sue descended with a rush.

The Old Doctor cleared his throat. Jane looked up with a start.

"Dr. Ed! For goodness' sake, come in!"

"Don't you dare tell me an old codger like me should have been home in bed an hour ago. I hear enough of that from Min Dawson. A regular jailer, that woman is."

"Now, Dr. Ed," as he came on into the office that until last spring had been his, "she's like the rest of us. She loves you."

The Old Doctor stood for a long minute, his eyes lingering on the ancient pigeonhole desk, only a bit less cluttered now than in his day, on the shining white and chrome and glass of the cabinets he could see through an open door, on Jane herself, sitting in the old swivel chair that had forgotten how to swivel a long time ago.

"Get up, Janie. Let's see if I still fit."

Jane rose, took the consulting chair that always was drawn up close.

With a contented sigh, Dr. Ed sat down. "Never thought I'd sit here again, Janie." He peered at her over his glasses. "What's keeping you so late tonight?"

"Nothing, really. I drove out to the Peterses'—Dr. Rinderle wants to examine Cynthia personally before he decides about an operation, and I—just stopped in."

The Old Doctor nodded. "I know. I used to do that when I was troubled."

He couldn't know that she had been sitting here thinking about Paul and Sue and herself. So he must think she was concerned about Cynthia. Jane didn't say anything.

They would have left the concert by now and would be at the Country Club. Dancing? Sue would be like a feather in Paul's arms; she would wear her happiness like an aura that would envelop them both—

Don't be a fool, Jane Langford! You're not in love with Paul . . .

CHAPTER 5

The doctors' lounge was not yet crowded, as it would be in a little while when the county medical society meeting got under way. Dr. Jane paused in the door.

"Good evening, everyone." She smiled around the pleasantly furnished room which had an air of spaciousness even if it was tucked in between Physical Therapy and Medical Records.

There were good evenings, spoken, grinned, or gestured.

"Didn't I see Hamlin with you?" Tom Winters moved over to make room for her on the cherry-red divan.

Jane nodded. "He ran into Jace Perry downstairs."

"Oh." And after a moment, "How does he like g. p. à la Halesville?"

"All right, I guess."

"Sometimes I get the feeling he thinks we're pretty small potatoes."

Jane did, too, but it was just Paul's way, she kept telling herself. Practice in a town as small as Halesville was still too new, and it was different from the ultra-ultra practice he had had in that New York suburb.

"—onto your hats, boys," Dr. Reynolds was saying. "Something tells me Laird is primed!"

"He walked past me a while ago like a wooden Indian making believe that wasn't a tomahawk in his hand." Dr. Jancieści groaned, "For lord's sake, it wasn't me!"

In the uncomfortable silence that lasted only a moment, Jancieski tapped a cigarette on his wrist before he put it between his lips. Of them all, the radiologist was the only one it couldn't possibly have been.

But which of the others? Reynolds . . . Miles . . . Winters . . . Fielding—

"Well," Dr. Jason Perry said from the doorway, "it's darn lucky the woman lived, is all I've got to say."

Jane found herself going around the room in her mind. It would be easy to imagine Jace Perry making a wrong diagnosis, which was what the rumors said had happened, and then bluffing it out. There wasn't a physician in this room, except Paul, who hadn't looked askance at the suave, Valentino-ish Dr. Jason Perry. And Paul would.

Andrews . . . O'Donnell . . . Meany— Her thoughts traveled on around the room.

Dr. Laird stalked in, and Jane saw what Dr. Jancieski meant when he said the chief of staff was "a wooden Indian making believe that wasn't a tomahawk." The cool blue eyes were absolutely flinty. His face was chiseled from granite, and looked just about as unyielding, as he crossed the lounge to a chair near the small kidney-shaped desk from which Dr. Fielding, as president of the society this year, would conduct the meeting.

John Reynolds was right, Jane found herself thinking. Dr. Laird was waiting only until he could see the whites of their eyes . . .

Then Dr. Fielding gave the glistening mahogany a single rap with his capped fountain pen, which had served the purpose ever since they couldn't find the gavel, and the meeting, always something less than formal, began.

The hospital was bulging at the seams. Did anybody have any ideas what could be done about it? How about petitioning the county commissioners? Wasn't that one way to start the ball rolling for a new addition?

"How do you think we'd staff it?" Dr. Winters demanded. "Miss Bond is always crying in her coffee for nurses, the way it is."

After they had mulled that over for a while, Dr. Fielding read a letter from the Martinsburg Woman's Club. The club wanted to do something for the hospital; they had raised over a thousand dollars and had planned a harvest festival for later this fall, and what would the hospital like to have?

"Sounds like this is our chance to start on that second emergency room," Dr. Fielding touched upon a sore subject with all of them, "but I suppose we should have a committee to talk it over with the ladies." He looked around the room. "Volunteers?"

Silence.

"All right then, nominations?"

"Winters," Dr. O'Donnell said.

"I resign. He's getting even because I think that pipe of his stinks."

In the general laughter somebody seconded. Somebody else nominated Hank Meany and Dr. Winters said, "I'll second that!"

"Paul Hamlin," Jane said.

Jace Perry seconded and the meeting moved on to other things. Should she ask for a committee to call on Clay Morton? Jane asked herself, and decided not to. At least not this time. Perhaps she could make him see, although after this afternoon it seemed hopeless.

It had been one of those slow afternoons in the office and on an impulse she had left the trickle of patients to Paul and driven out to the factory.

Yes, Mr. Morton was in, Mary Ames, his secretary, told her. No, she didn't think he was too busy to see her.

If Dr. Jane would sit down, please, she would see—

Jane thanked her. But she didn't take one of the beige leather chairs along the wall. Instead, she went to the window and stood looking up at the towering stacks—and at the smoke besmirching the last-of-September sky as it drifted on a lazy wind.

Mrs. Woods was better today, thank goodness. If only they could get that place in the country—

"This way, Dr. Jane."

Miss Ames opened a door and stood aside for her to enter. "Dr. Langford, Mr. Morton."

"Well, Dr. Langford." Clay Morton's smile was as pompous as the rest of him. He motioned her to a chair, not beige but dark red. "To what do I owe the pleasure?"

Jane sat down. "I'm afraid it isn't going to be a pleasure, Mr. Morton."

"My smoke again, eh? I heard Amelia Woods had another spell with her asthma, so"—he fixed her on the pale of his animosity—"I figured you'd be around. I can always tell, Dr. Langford."

Already the breath of defeat was cold on the back of her neck. Jane could feel it, could see that defeat in the man's aloof arrogance as he leaned back in the handsome red leather executive's chair and folded his arms across his paunch.

"I'm sorry about Amelia, Dr. Langford. But I wouldn't borrow trouble if I were you."

That was all she could get out of him. "His people" were living better than they ever had lived in their lives. Surely she didn't seriously believe they held him responsible for small, infrequent discomforts?

A discreet nudge from Dr. Winters brought her back to the present.

Dr. Laird had risen, was sweeping the lounge with those

cool, dispassionate eyes. If I were the one, Jane thought, and then didn't finish it.

"While we have nearly everybody here, I have a few words—"

Carefully chosen words, Jane could see. Dr. Laird paused. Again he looked around the room, his gaze touching all of them—and lingering longest on whom? Someone's chair fidgeted, the Woman's Club letter in Dr. Fielding's hand rustled. He laid it down.

"The other night," Dr. Laird continued, "a man named Thomas Jennings called Dr. Andrews. His wife was ill. She had been ill since early evening, suffering abdominal pains, vomiting, the pain becoming severe and moving from the pit of the stomach to the lower right abdominal area—"

For heaven's sake! Jane thought. Who could fail to diagnose *that*?

Dr. Laird spoke unhurriedly, measuring each word and gauging its impact on his listeners. Dr. Andrews' face was a mask. Jane wished she could see Dr. Winters', but she couldn't.

Dr. O'Donnell stopped torturing his jaw with his fist. Jace Perry studied his thumbnail, became conscious that he was, raised his eyes to Dr. Laird's face.

His lips thinning with the distaste of what he was about to say, the chief of staff told them the rest of it. "They were in a motel several miles from Martinsburg. He didn't have much money, just enough to get them back to Akron—himself, his wife and three small children. He had told the other doctor that. Would Dr. Andrews come? The other doctor wouldn't—"

In the stunned stillness, the wintry eyes combed the room again. For a sign of guilt? Or was the man who only called himself a doctor here? They never had one hundred per cent attendance at their meetings.

"'You'd better get somebody else,' Jennings said he was told." Dr. Laird paused, to let that register. "The woman lived, although with rupture and peritonitis, it was nip and tuck for a while.

"And perhaps I would have been hard put to prove malpractice if she hadn't"—anger long suppressed roughened the doctor's voice now—"but by the Lord Harry I'd have tried! And I shall try if such a thing ever comes to my attention again.

"I'm naming no names. But the doctor is a member of

this Society and that makes it the responsibility of the Society and of each of us as individuals."

Dr. Laird sat down.

For moments that seemed long there was silence, that absolute stillness that is shock, disbelief. None of us would, Jane thought.

Not even Jace Perry—

Then Dr. Fielding rapped the desk top with his pen. He cleared his throat, glanced around the room, clearly at a loss.

"Well—" he began finally.

Jace Perry stopped twirling his thumbs. "How can we be sure the guy is telling the truth? He could have been trying to arouse sympathy and no doubt a little ready cash."

Again that uncomfortable quiet, although Dr. Andrews' nostrils flared with the sharp, angry intake of breath.

"It could be, you know," Perry reminded them reasonably.

Dr. Laird answered him in that same slow, measured verbal tread with which he had recounted the incident. "I think Jennings is telling the truth, all right. And he has not asked for charity. He has a job waiting for him in Akron. He will pay his bills."

Jace Perry shrugged.

"If there's nothing else?" Dr. Fielding's hope that there wasn't was obvious.

Surely it wasn't he! Jane thought, startled, because it might be. *Several miles from Martinsburg—* Dr. Fielding practiced in Woodbine, which was fifteen or sixteen miles.

But then, by that deduction, it also could be Hank Meany, or Dr. Grayling, who wasn't here tonight, or Paul, or— A tremor went through her. Were some of the rest of them thinking that, too? That it might have been she?

Hank Meany rose. "I think there is something else." He dropped a bill on the kidney-shaped desk. A ten. "Those kids have got to eat."

Jane had lain for hours, it seemed, tossing, unable to sleep. What was the matter with her, anyway? It was utterly useless to live over again and again in her thoughts that night the woman had been brought to the hospital. That told her nothing, except that Dr. Winters very likely knew *who*. And that Miss Delman might know.

The woman sobbing . . . the tortured man who ordered coffee and "hamburger—anything" in the restaurant across the street. She knew now that he had been Thomas Jennings, worried sick—and no wonder.

She pummeled her pillow again and then didn't lie on it. Hugging the blanket around her knees, she sat up. It wasn't she and it wasn't Paul—that was all that mattered, really. Let Jace Perry violate the precepts he had sworn to uphold if he wanted to—it was his to answer for.

After a time, Jane slipped out of bed. The bare, polished walnut boards were cold beneath her feet as she went to the window and stood looking out. It wasn't fair that she always came back to Dr. Perry, although she couldn't imagine any of the others saying to a frantic man whose wife was desperately ill, "You'd better get someone else." Worriedly, Jane let her forehead rest against the cool pane.

The cloud that had been hiding the moon went scudding past, and the tall, thin spire of Bill's church gleamed palely through the black lace that was the boughs of the elms in the yard. What a sermon Bill could preach on this thing! Jane could see him, firm, long-fingered hands gripping either side of the pulpit as he leaned forward, intense, angry because it was not God's way, that anger burning like fires deep in his smoke-gray eyes—

"Bill."

Her voice was soft as the night.

Bill was wrong. Sue Latham was thinking as she walked along Main Street. She could be happy in Halesville. Very happy—now that Paul was here.

Before that, though— Sue wrinkled her nose with the spatter of freckles marching in ragged formation, like retreating Confederates, Paul teased her. Before that, Halesville had been all right for people like Bill and Jane and Dr. Ed, the old darling. They needed to be needed. Oh, so do I! Sue thought now, happily. But by Paul, not the whole darn town and half the county.

She waved at Mr. Bates, who was putting new magazines on the display rack near the drugstore window. Mr. Bates was like Jane and Dr. Ed. And Bill, naturally. People were always leaning on preachers and doctors and druggists. Telling them all sorts of things, Paul said.

Passing the small white building where he and Jane had their offices, she wondered if he was there now. It wasn't office hours, but he might be.

No, his car wasn't there. Neither was Jane's. Calls, calls, calls. Worse than being a preacher, being a doctor was.

She smiled at nothing in particular. A doctor's wife had to get used to calls at all hours and any hour. Look at Jane, dashing off in the middle of supper or at bedtime—or dawn. Or in between. What a life Jane and Bill were going to have.

She wasn't in love with Paul, Sue had decided. Not yet. But she might be.

And who knew? Lightning might strike and Paul would fall in love with her. She would know when he did, if he did, before he knew it himself, probably.

When he looked at her the way he sometimes looked at Jane—

Sue stooped to pick up a maple leaf that was golden perfection. She walked on, twirling it rapidly between thumb and forefinger and watching the darkening and lightening of the blur as it spun.

She should be home raking the yard. Or setting the rest of the Old Doctor's bulbs where he wanted them. She had the ground ready, a patch here, a triangle there, one for the red, another for the pink parrots, an oblong for the clusters that would bloom golden, white, just about every other tulip color come spring.

She loved doing it, hearing the Old Doctor say, "A dozen white parrots for here" . . . "Save the pink Empress, Sue. Min wants them where she can see them from the kitchen windows." . . . "There goes Janie hustling out to the car. Wonder who—"

The old dear. His heart was still in that pill bag no matter how cranky it was.

Idly, she let the maple leaf go and stood watching it flutter and swoop and be wafted gently down until it poised, seeming to await the perfect ripple before it settled on the water.

Today was a day for leaning on bridge railings and watching the shallow water in the river play with the pebbles and the occasional broken reed that went drifting by, she thought after a time. No fish today, though, although sometimes she saw them. A funny flat sunfish, or a school of tiny minnows darting hither and yon . . .

The truck was rattling the rickety bridge before she was aware of it. Oh, she'd heard it approaching, she supposed, but the sound had remained on the periphery of her daydream and not until it stopped and Larry Burton sang out,

"Like a lift back to town, lady?" did she really care who it was.

"Why, Larry! Hello!"

She hopped into the cab beside him, being careful to watch out for the spring that was nudging through the worn upholstery. If he got a good crop next year, Larry was going to buy another truck, not a new one, for he still needed tools to farm with, but a good second-hand one.

"Ran out of fertilizer, darn it," he grumbled, as he shifted the noisy gears. And when they were under way, "What were you thinking about back there? You were a couple of million miles away."

Sue shook her head. "Nothing, I guess. At least nothing much. Dr. Ed's tulip bulbs, and there aren't any fish today." She stole a glance at him. "Things like that, I guess."

"You're doing a lot of guessing."

She was. Too much. But Larry would whoop if she told him she had been thinking about Paul.

He parked in front of the drugstore. "Afraid a Coke will spoil your lunch?" And before she could say no, it wouldn't, "There's Doc Hamlin. Zoweeee! What a flivver!"

Paul had just turned onto Main and was coming toward them. He was going to stop—

"A beeyewtee," Larry whistled, "but not for Burton. Not even when I get that land built up. For Pete's sake, I could buy a new tractor and plows and—"

But Sue could hardly hear him, her heart was thudding so. So love was like this. Your heart telling you and the whole world, it seemed, shouting it from the housetops. Surely Paul must hear, and Larry—

"Sue," Paul said.

In a special special way? Or was she only imagining tenderness in his voice because she wanted to hear it there?

"Hi, Burton," Paul said then to Larry. "How's the sowing and reaping?"

"So-so."

"Larry's in to get more fertilizer. He ran out." Sue didn't quite know why she explained Larry's presence but she had, and Paul said, "Oh, I see."

Larry gave them a funny look. "Well—"

His grin had a sort of wobbly look to it, and Sue wondered if he was working too hard.

"I'm glad I ran into you, Sue. Good to see you again, Doc," and the door slammed behind him. The motor coughed and then roared.

He was going to buy me a Coke, Sue remembered suddenly.

"If I interrupted something, I'm sorry." Paul was looking down at her, not quite smiling.

Sue shook her head.

CHAPTER 6

The mellow, golden days were slipping past. Already it was the middle of October and, almost daily, wedges of wild geese were overhead, headed south. Sometimes there were ducks, strung out behind their leader, and once, returning in the dawn from a night call, Jane saw a flock riding at anchor on a farmer's pond, one venerable drake with neck stretched tall, his handsome green and blue and black head turning alertly this way and that as he paddled around his sleeping charges.

She stopped the car and sat for a long time, watching, until finally, as if at some prearranged time and signal, the flock rose with a whirrrr-rrr, some circling, dipping playfully, lagging, but not for long. The sentinel drake exhorted, threatened, cajoled, until the ranks closed up and they were off. With a feeling of sadness, Jane punched the starter button.

Most of Halesville was awake, or wakening. It was a town of early risers, for the day shift at Morton's went on at seven and many others drove to plants, offices and stores in Martinsburg.

Although she had been up for hours, Dr. Jane's own day would "begin" after breakfast and a shower. Granny would be up—she always was when Jane returned from these night calls—and there would be hot cocoa or hot milk, or coffee, depending on what time it was.

This morning, Jane thought fondly, it would be coffee. And, she hoped, wheat cakes and sausages. Until now, with tantalizing breakfasty smells teasing her nostrils, she hadn't realized how hungry she was.

Sleepy, too, she thought, yawning. Maybe she would take the shower before breakfast, a cold one. That way she could dawdle over her coffee and listen to Granny's account of Ladies' Aid which had met all day yesterday to clean the church. If they didn't do something about that carpet pretty soon, they were going to have Granny to answer to.

"Good morning, Granny," Jane called from the front door. She set her bag on the drum table. "I'll shower and be right down. Could we have wheat cakes and sausage?"

Granny-sounds, as Sue called the snatches of hymns and talking to herself, came from the kitchen. Granny appeared in the door.

"A body'd think that was Bill Latham askin' for wheat cakes and sausage." She rested thin, gnarled fingers on the banister. "I hope he's gittin' 'em," she added wistfully.

Jane leaned over the banister to kiss the wrinkled forehead. "Not your wheat cakes, Granny darling."

The old woman's eyes were misty, and so were Jane's as she ran up the walnut stairs. Granny missed Bill dreadfully. And she worried about him—more than was good for her, Jane suspected when, on occasion, Granny pulled the walls of her world up close.

Africa was a world away, out of the world—*her* world, it seemed sometimes—

It was an unhappy Jane Langford who regarded her from the mirror as, minutes later, she buttoned her fresh crisp white blouse and tucked it in. What was happening to her and Bill?

Or at least, to her?

The hazel eyes in the mirror asked the question and she couldn't answer it.

Although it had buzzed madly for days after Dr. Laird lashed out at the still-unnamed doctor, the hospital at Martinsburg was back to normal now. The Jenningses had gone on to Akron, and there was new fuel for the grapevine: Jenny Akers had caught "her" orderly smooching with one of the senior students and had *she* ever told *him* off! The student, too, although Jenny had confided she couldn't blame the girl for falling for Guy.

Crossing the foyer now, Dr. Jane smiled at the memory and at the girl, not Jenny who worked nights, who was busy with a call at the switchboard. Jane touched the button to bring the elevator down.

Mrs. Elder, who was going to have a thyroidectomy as soon as they could get her heart settled down, would be waiting . . . The elevator came, discharged an aide who had been distributing the morning mail and a medical technologist with a tray of vials, alcohol, sterile cotton and syringes. Blood specimens for analysis, Jane identified the girl's mission without really thinking about it.

She got in the elevator, punched "2" and rode up.

"Just look, Dr. Jane!" Mrs. Elder waved a plump hand over the cards spread in colorful array over her bed. "A regular shower of them! Isn't it thrilling?"

"Goodness, yes." Jane noted the flush that tinted her patient's skin, and the short, quick breaths. Mrs. Elder knew excitement was bad for her. "That's a pretty one."

"Isn't it?" The woman eyed the stethoscope Jane had taken from her bag. Her smile was touched with worry. "I'm being naughty, I know."

"A little, I'm afraid."

After examining Mrs. Elder, Jane saw two or three other patients, waved good morning to Tom Winters, who was hurrying toward o. b., stopped to talk for a few minutes with Miss Lancaster, who had transferred to day duty and who was anxious about Cynthia Peters.

"She's going back to City in November, Miss Lancaster," Jane told her. "Dr. Rinderle and Dr. Warren hope to operate then. They're very hopeful."

"I'm glad," the nurse said warmly. "She's the bravest child!"

Jane nodded. "I'll tell her you asked about her," she promised.

She was leaving the hospital when Dr. Laird hailed her.

"Dr. Langford! Have you a minute?"

"Of course, Doctor."

Dr. Jane had expected to walk beside the chief of staff, or follow his arrow-straight, white-clad back along the corridor to his cubbyhole of an office; instead, Dr. Laird was crossing the foyer to her.

"How is Dr. Johnson these days? I've been meaning to ask you."

They walked outside and stood for a few minutes talking about the Old Doctor who, Jane said she felt, was finding it difficult to accustom himself to the slow pace of retirement.

"I suppose we all will," Dr. Laird said.

Jane nodded.

The surgeon squinted at the wisp of cloud that momentarily darkened the sun. "Hope this weather holds. I'd like to get down to the Smokies for a couple of days this weekend."

"I hope you can."

"Oh, we probably won't. Helen says just let us plan something and Look Out!"

Jane laughed. "I'll tell my patients. No emergencies until Monday."

"You do that."

Chuckling, Dr. Laird went back inside and Jane walked around to the doctors' parking area wondering why she had felt a moment's malaise at Dr. Laird's "Dr. Langford!" Because she had been thinking this morning about the Jennings family?

A handful of student nurses came out of the Students' Building, glanced her way, and went on, chattering. About last night's date or someone's "afternoon," probably.

Or, Jane thought with a private smile, Jenny's orderly.

She got in her car, backed, and then waited while an ambulance crept along the driveway. Dr. Meany's car was right behind.

Hank Meany had been awfully quick to start that fund for the Jennings kids—

Paul had said that once when they were talking about it. "A suspicious mind might almost infer conscience."

"Paul!" Jane had cried, shocked. "Hank wouldn't."

"Okay. So Hank wouldn't." Paul shook his head at her. "Wise up, Jane. Hank Meany's no angel. And we all make mistakes."

Remembering now as she waved to Hank and drove out into the street, Jane wished she hadn't. That they hadn't resurrected the Jennings episode at all. After all, it was past and no doubt the doctor involved had sweat blood and fear —yes, and conscience—many hours.

But Paul had been to one of those committee meetings with Dr. Winters and Dr. Meany and somehow they had got to talking about Hank—

Prospects looked good for the second emergency room. The Woman's Club was enthusiastic and hoped to enlist Kiwanis and Rotary . . . Determinedly, Jane tooled her thoughts into pleasanter channels.

Back in Halesville a little later, she picked up her mail, exchanged remarks about the weather with Sam Christy as she riffled through it. A medical journal, bills for surgical dressings and that new ophthalmoscope—she identified them by their return addresses. One envelope that might contain a check. A very feminine-smelling letter for Paul. Lilac?

The black bag was her badge of authority. People stepped back. Somebody yelled, "Here's a doctor!" and the echo was a fervent "Thank God!" that was almost a moan.

"Over here, Dr. Langford," the state policeman called.

He and another man were on their knees beside a third, who was hemorrhaging from a bad wound on his thigh. The femoral artery? Direct pressure— Swiftly Jane located the artery above the injury and pressed the heel of her hand on it—hard.

The bleeding slowed . . . and stopped, and with her other hand, Jane sought the man's pulse. Too fast.

Shock—

"Get blankets and pillows," she ordered.

The state policeman sprang up.

"What about the others?" Jane asked the other man. She did not look up. She was working swiftly, surely.

"Broken arms and legs, mostly. Some cuts. There's one"—he swallowed—"killed."

Only one? Jane thought with the part of her mind that wasn't concentrating on the job at hand. Somehow she would have expected more.

"In the car?"

The man said, "Yeah. He was driving," indicating her patient.

After that they didn't talk. The policeman brought blankets collected from goodness only knew whose cars or the motel nearby and a seat from the police car. They had the man wrapped and in shock position when another police car came shrieking. A woman was crooning softly to her baby; a child who also had been a passenger on the bus began crying again, and the driver, nursing his broken arm the best he could, tried to comfort her—

"My God, why don't they hurry?"

But it hadn't been the eon it seemed and already the banshee shriek of sirens could be heard, faint and miles away but rapidly loudening. Jane's eyes went again to the shock victim, ashy looking, not quite unconscious but not conscious, either.

She couldn't be three places at once and she needed to be.

"Lordy, what a session!"

Dr. Reynolds ran long, nervous fingers through his salt-and-pepper hair. "If the good ladies of the Woman's Club could have seen this, we'd get that new emergency room for sure. You must tell them, Hamlin."

"I shall," Paul promised. "With vivid adjectives and buckets of blood."

It was hours later. Broken bones, cuts and contusions, the more serious injuries, had been take care of. Paul had come directly to the hospital when Clara Mae Oley located him, and now he, Jane, and Dr. Reynolds were leaving the hospital via the ambulance entrance which the doctors used more than they did the front door.

"Things like this"—Dr. Reynolds ground clenched fists futilely into trouser pockets. "Senseless slaughter! Nothing more, nothing less!"

"Yes," Paul agreed with him. "But so long as there is one person in the world, Reynolds, there will be senselessness."

A few steps in silence; then, "I suppose so." The fierce anger because it was true and there was nothing he could do to change it returned to Dr. Reynolds' voice. "But you don't have to be so damned philosophical about it!"

Paul burst out laughing. "Sorry, Reynolds. I guess I did sound that way, didn't I?"

They had arrived at the physicians' parking area and Dr. Reynolds said, chuckling, "Forget it. As Jancieski would say, Reynolds on his soapbox."

He walked around Dr. Laird's car to his own.

"As Reynolds just said," Paul paraphrased, "Lordy, what a session!" He cupped Jane's elbow in his hand. "How about steak and French fries?"

"With apple pie and cheese?"

"Dr. Langford," he said solemnly, "you read my mind." And with a sigh, "I suppose we shall have to let Mrs. Mason know where . . . The club?"

"All right."

They hadn't been to the Country Club since that evening the gypsy girl sang her disturbingly beautiful love songs, nor had either of them mentioned their sudden departure. As she leaned back against the crimson plaid upholstery of Paul's car, Jane wondered if he were thinking of it now.

She stole a glance at him, but he was concentrating on his driving. Or at least not wearing his thoughts on his sleeve. With a gusty little sigh, she closed her eyes.

"Tired?" Paul asked gently.

"A little."

The wind in her hair, chill and yet soft against her eyelids and cheeks—

Then it was Paul's lips brushing her cheek, lightly, tenderly, so lightly and tenderly she might have imagined the kiss.

"Paul—"

He didn't say anything.

"—you shouldn't."

They had stopped for a light and heads had turned to admire the long, low convertible, pale silver in the glow from the street lamps—and stayed turned. Jane felt her cheeks flushing.

Then the light flipped to green and as the big car was wafted forward, Paul said, "If you expect me to say I'm sorry, I'm not. I had to do that, Jane. You don't know how you looked—leaning back there, your eyes closed, lips parted. I—Jane—"

She didn't look at him. "I'm beginning to see what you meant when you said you would tell the Woman's Club in quote vivid adjectives unquote."

"Stop changing the subject."

Another light, but they were farther apart now. Then the outskirts of town were whirling backward past them again. Ahead, the highway wore a strand of headlights.

Paul had kissed her . . . only it hadn't been a kiss and it didn't mean a thing. Why, then, was her heart hammering away like mad? Jane drew a deep, steadying breath. She should say something, laugh it off—only she couldn't.

And that was wrong. She was going to marry Bill. She would tell Paul tonight.

The car barely slowed, and whirled into the driveway marked "PRIVATE" that led half a mile back to the Country Club.

"Jane—"

Halfway up the drive, he let the car roll to a halt. "I—meant it back there, Jane. I had to kiss you." He drew her, unprotesting, to him. "I have to—now," as his mouth claimed hers.

CHAPTER 7

Paul, please—

But the protest was only in her heart.

"Oh, Paul!" It was a whisper, scarcely audible, wrenched from her.

His mouth came down again, in a hard, demanding kiss. "Jane—" He kissed her again, lingeringly. "That's how it is with me, darling."

Jane shook her head. It couldn't be. Her lips felt as if they belonged to someone else . . . Her heart?

"Paul—"

"Don't say it."

"I've got to, Paul. There's—Bill."

Bill— Her heart gave a sick, crazy lurch. She was in love with Bill—of course she was!

"You're not in love with him. You just think you are. Or thought you were." Paul grinned at her. "After the way you kissed me, let's get our tenses straight."

She had difficulty disentangling her eyes from his. No! She couldn't fall out of love so easily—not the kind of love she had felt for Bill—

Had felt? Didn't she feel it now?

Joe Hiram's neighbors looked out for their own. On a bright day when October was giving way to November they descended on the Hiram fields, cornpickers, tractors, wagons, men. And women. For at noon, tables made of long, wide boards across sawhorses fairly groaned, they were so loaded with food.

Although by now she had become accustomed to church suppers and the town picnic which was held each August, and the spring festival, Jane Langford thought she never had seen anything like it. Baked chicken and dressing, fried chicken, ham and brown gravy, mashed potatoes beaten fluffy and white, pies baked from pumpkins grown in the corn and on those husky wedges of pie, tall, quivering mounds of whipped cream.

"Just look at my plate! Granny won't have to cook for a week."

Sue managed a sadness. "Just think what Bed Forrest could have done with all this."

"Whipped the Yankees?" Larry Burton teased.

"Oh you—you *Yankee!*"

"My great-grandpa was, and I reckon there were times when this ham and gravy would've tasted mighty good to him."

"When General Forrest was running him out of Tennessee, no doubt."

Jane laughed. "All right, you two. Truce?"

"Why?" Sue demanded. "He's a da—"

Larry popped a piece of candied pear into her mouth, and amid the general laughter someone began singing in a full-bodied bass, "The years creep slowly by, Lorena—"

It was that kind of day. Lighthearted. Happy. Because a man might have lost an arm, or his life, and hadn't. Of course they didn't know, yet, whether Joe Hiram would ever use his hand again, but the shadow lay only in Dr. Jane's thoughts and, perhaps, in Joe Hiram's

A new crispness was in the air these days. Although the sunshine lay warm and golden across field and woods, there was a promise of gray, melancholy days ahead. The rains would be welcome to these farmers, Jane thought, because the autumn had been too dry for comfort. Even now she could look out across a field sown with wheat and see dust devils bobbing and swirling and pirouetting in impish glee.

"There's weather brewing." Joe Hiram sat down beside her.

Jane smiled. "You can feel it in your bones, I suppose? That's what Mrs. Neidlinger was just telling me a while ago."

The farmer grinned. "Aunt Sibbie's a card. As a matter of fact, I heard it on the morning news. Rain beginning tomorrow. A rainy spell, thank the Lord."

"It's lucky you're getting your corn picked today, then."

Joe Hiram glanced down at the two fingers and a thumb peeking from bandages that swathed his hand and arm. "I'm a pretty lucky guy, Dr. Jane," he said softly. "But I guess you know that."

Silently Jane nodded.

"I won't be forgetting it." Joe Hiram gave her a level look. "I guess you know that, too."

"None of us will," the man who had piloted the Jeep on that wild ride through pasture and field chimed in. "Anything we can do, ma'am, you just say the word and it's done." Reaching for another wedge of pie, he added with a grin, "Good as, anyways."

Jane thanked him just as tiny Mrs. Neidlinger descended, her indignation unfurled like a battle banner. "Get outen that pie, Jack Simmons! That's four pieces!"

"Now, Aunt Sibbie—" Joe Hiram began.

"I don't care! *Four* pieces!"

Jack Simmons winked at Jane. "Oh well, if I get the gout, Doc Jane'll fix me up. Won't you, Doc?"

"Reckon she will." Aunt Sibbie was still simmering. "She ain't like that doctor ever'body's talkin' about." Her indignation was mounting again. "Refusin' to go to see that pore woman! An' her dyin' with cancer! I declare, I never heerd the likes of—"

"She had appendicitis, Mrs. Neidlinger," Dr. Jane interrupted quietly.

"No matter. He didn't go."

Jane drew a deep breath. Aunt Sibbie Neidlinger was right. The ailment didn't matter. Any doctor who was a doctor would have gone—as Dr. Andrews had.

Mrs. Neidlinger peered at her. "I don't reckon you got any idear who it was?"

"No, I haven't."

Jane might have known the story would get out. It was the kind of thing that did, and then it snowballed before it burst into many tiny stones that promptly began to gather gossip and grow and grow—

"I don't mean to be rude, Aunt Sibbie," she added. "It's just that I don't even *want* to know."

The old woman patted her shoulder, gave a last warning to Jack Simmons, who was eyeing the pumpkin pie again, and went bustling off.

"Don't mind Aunt Sibbie," Joe Hiram said. "She's got to have her say."

"I know." Jane summoned a smile she did not feel.

Jack Simmons scooped up another piece of pie. "Well, that was a raw deal. Whoever."

"Yes," Jane agreed.

But, she wondered later, as she drove back toward Halesville, why had she felt as if she were on trial?

Not even Mrs. Neidlinger, with all her vehemence, had meant anything. It was just that a physician swore to do all in his power to relieve suffering and here was one who didn't, which shocked—and *shook*—their trust.

The rain which the weather bureau and Aunt Sibbie Neidlinger's "j'ints" predicted began the next day and now, days later, it showed no signs of letting up. Oh, it didn't rain continuously—sometimes it didn't rain for a whole day, or there would be a slow, steady drizzle instead of the pelting, bone-chilling storm that had begun at noon.

It must be colder, Jane thought. Or else she had caught the 'flu bug that had laid Amelia Woods low.

She sat for a long time watching the raindrops spatter on the high clerestory windows. An east wind, raw, penetrating— She shivered again, just thinking about it.

The waiting room was empty and apt to stay that way, an afternoon like this. And with Paul in Stewart—

For which she was glad, in a way, Jane told herself. She needed to think . . . She was going to have to make up her mind about Paul.

Either she was in love with him or she wasn't. With Paul there could be no in-between—he loved her, he wanted her. And, he insisted, she felt the same way about him. If she didn't, she would have gone to Bill Latham long ago.

Remembering, Jane bit her lip. Was he right? Had her feeling for Bill been a reach for the security that love brought a woman—a salve for her ego after Lance? Paul said that it was.

After a long time, she rose from the Old Doctor's battered rolltop desk and went into the examining room. She could check supplies and get off an order—Paul hated doing things like that.

Just as he would hate sitting alone in that cubbyhole office in Stewart waiting for patients who today would stay at home unless they were too sick to wait for the rain to slacken. And then they would telephone . . . Smiling a little at the thought of Paul fuming and not knowing what to do with himself, or sloshing off in answer to an urgent call, Jane opened a supply cabinet and ran a practiced eye over its contents.

Medications, gauze, sterile dressings—the four-by-fours were getting low. And plaster of Paris. Although there was enough for several more casts, you never could tell . . . She was standing at a window, the list in her hand, when the door opened.

Dropping the list on her desk as she passed, Jane hurried into the waiting room.

"Why, Dr. Perry! Good afternoon."

Jace Perry flipped rain off his gray felt. "Good afternoon my foot. Paul around?"

"He's in Stewart."

"Till five?"

With a glance at the wall clock, Jane nodded.

Perry's glance followed hers. "Three twenty-one," he said musingly. "Think I'll drive over." He grinned at her. "If you're expecting him for dinner, don't."

"I wasn't."

"Thought you might be."

Insolent eyes traveled over her and Jane felt her flesh creep. This man a *doctor?*

"Dr. Perry—"

Forefinger wagging playfully, Jace Perry cautioned, "Anh-anh, sweetheart. If I miss Paul, tell him to call me, will you?"

"Why should you miss him? We keep office hours until five."

"Oh," with that eloquent shrug of his, "an emergency. A house call. In this weather anything can happen."

He was right . . . and she had been wrong to let him needle her. Jace Perry wouldn't forget.

"Rock of Ages, Cleft for me, Let me hide myself In Theeee—"

Granny Mason's thin soprano held onto the note and it comforted her. A song like that gave a body somethin' to cling to, she'd always told the preacher, "the preacher" to Granny being Bill Latham, not the young ministerial student who was supplying the church while Bill was gone. He agreed with her, too, Bill Latham did, and he was teachin' their songs to them natives— Granny hid a sigh behind a few bars of "Rock of Ages." It was going to be lonesome in this big old house when Dr. Jane and Sue both went up to Central City, but Granny was glad they were going. Dr. Jane needed to get away, if only for three or four days.

And Granny had an idea Sue Latham did, too. She'd catch her, sometimes when she thought a body wasn't lookin', that pretty face of hers all clouded up, and her eyes— Granny shook her head. Eatin' her heart out, the girl was.

Granny had an idea what it was, too, or rather, *who* it was, and she didn't like it. Not one *little* bit, she was telling herself hotly when the telephone rang.

"Dr. Langford's res'dence," she said into the kitchen extension.

"Know where Janie is, Melviny?"

Uneasiness jabbed through Granny Mason at the excitement in the Old Doctor's voice. Ed Johnson knowed better than to let himself get upset like that—

"She was goin' to the Woodses' and out to the Paytons' to see the baby—" She rattled off two or three more calls Jane had intended to make tonight because she was going to Central City early in the morning.

The Old Doctor grunted. "Well, ne' mind."

"Ed Johnson, you all right?"

"Tut, Melviny. Don't get your bile in an uproar. What makes you think I'm not?"

He hung up before she could tell him.

The familiar corridors with muted green walls and cork-tiled floors, miles of them, stacked tier on tier, it used to seem when she had been on duty here. New faces, and a few that she recognized. Dr. Warren's of course—she'd already talked with him. And with Dr. Rinderle, who with Dr. Warren and City's crack surgical team was going to operate on Cynthia day after tomorrow.

And Clem Bartlett . . . She hadn't realized how glad she was going to be to see Clem, how hungry she had been for talk of their internship when Clem, Peter Farley, and she had paired off two at a time for night ambulance duty, the emergency rooms, the big, overflowing free clinic.

As she stooped to drink from one of the sixth-floor water coolers Dr. Jane smiled to herself. Could it be that she had been just a little homesick for sprawling, bustling City Hospital?

She drank, and walked on. Past the nurses' station, past doors opening into rooms painted the same soft shade of green. Jane supposed the patients didn't mind, it was a nice green, but she preferred variety, the pale pinks, the quiet blues, the warm, sunshiny yellows in which the rooms at the hospital in Martinsburg were done.

"Dr. Jane!"

The surprised, glad yelp came from behind her. Jane turned.

"Emily Evans!" she cried, as gladly. "Gracious, I'm glad to see you! But—here?"

The nurse who had been on night duty at Dr. MacAllen Randall's exclusive Randall's Convalescent Hospital when Jane was on the staff those two years echoed, "Here. I've been at

City almost a year, Dr. Jane. Private duty mostly, but right now I'm on the floor. Have you seen Dr. Mac?"

"Not yet."

But she would. Also Dr. Louise . . . and Lance, although she wasn't too sure that Lance Hart would be pleased to see her. She glanced down at the tray of medications the nurse was carrying.

"I mustn't keep you, Emily. I'm having dinner with Dr. Bartlett—we went through med school and interned together—but lunch tomorrow?"

They made the date, for a late lunch just before Emily went on duty at three, and Jane hurried on. If she didn't run, she wouldn't be ready when Clem and that young intern for Sue came.

Central City hadn't changed, Jane decided the next day. It was still noisy—"sprawl-y and brawl-y," Peter Farley used to say on nights when they got more than their share of cracked heads in Emergency. Cars still charged the traffic signals and tires still screeched and horns still blared, policemen's whistles shrilled just as piercingly, you still got jostled and shoved and walked past as though you weren't there . . . and it was still wonderful.

"Oh Jane, look—"

Sue had stopped in front of Bard's. "Look at that fabulous gown!"

"You should have had that last night."

"With my funny nose and freckles?" The freckles changed formation when Sue grinned.

Jane said laughingly, "On second thought, I think the dress would have been wasted. Dr. Hanna could hardly take his eyes off you, anyway."

She studied the gown a moment. Ivory velveteen with a high, demure neck and a snug bodice, a skirt that was gracefully full. "Want to try it on?"

Sue shook her head.

They went into Bard's, anyway. And to three or four other stores. The bundles began to pile up. A warm woolen stole for Granny. A muffler and a cap with ear muffs so that the Old Doctor could take his "morning constitutionals" when the weather got bad, Sue said. Kid gloves for Mrs. Dawson, the Old Doctor's housekeeper.

A knitted suit for Jane, a sort of frosty blue that com-

hands that had delivered he had forgotten how many babies and had patched up myriad cuts and broken bones, hands clasped now in the old familiar "Here's the church, here's the steeple—" Jane waited. The Old Doctor had something on his mind. Bill, she was almost sure.

Well, he had to know. He had a *right* to know.

"Janie," the Old Doctor began after a time, and then was silent for so long she thought he had changed his mind. The worried eyes came back from the window, darkening now as the November dusk sifted down. "Janie, about Paul Hamlin—"

Her breath caught. He knew already; she might have known she couldn't fool Dr. Ed.

"Are you in love with him, Janie?"

The Old Doctor's voice was tired, as drawn as his face. Sudden alarm stabbed through her. He was actually *gray!*

"Sue told you?"

"I've got eyes, Janie. And ears."

People *would* talk, Jane thought. Sue had said they were talking . . .

"Well, Janie?" the Old Doctor prompted finally.

"I don't know, Dr. Ed. I'm—not sure."

Something must have happened to the calendar. Here it was Thanksgiving already, and it couldn't be. The days couldn't have gone by that fast. But they had. Bill Latham regarded today—Thanksgiving Day, it said in red letters—in the log he had kept since his first day at the little mission station, and shook his head.

It was high time he was looking to Christmas. These kids hadn't been singing "Away in a Manger" and "Hark! the Herald Angels Sing" since they could talk, as his Sunday school in Halesville had, but kids the world over loved pageantry. A cantata would be just the thing.

With that wizened little nephew of Asey-for-short's as Joseph—

The preacher nodded his satisfaction at the inspired thought. The boy had Asey-for-short worried, and Asey should know the pitfalls, Bill thought. He had been in enough of them.

Leaning back in his reed chair, Bill Latham let his mind explore the cantata idea. The songs would be easy. His people had a natural sense of rhythm—all of the natives seemed to have—and they were quick to learn. Look at the way Keaa

Not even the dull hummmm, she realized suddenly. The line was dead.

"The storm has broken the line." She was grateful for her years of training, the discipline that kept her voice level, unworried. "You'll have to go."

Jim Ludlow nodded, and while he pulled on arctics and mackinaw she told him what she wanted. Oxygen equipment and a nurse skilled in its use. He was to get hold of Dr. Thomas Winters, or if he couldn't locate Dr. Winters, Dr. Laird.

"Here"—hurriedly she scribbled on one of her prescription sheets—"in case there are doubts."

The man thrust the sheet into a pocket. "Amy," to his wife. He held her a moment and over her head his anxious eyes asked a question.

"I'll stay," Jane answered it.

The storm was getting worse. By midafternoon, wind came questing through the snow, gently at first as though it sought something lost. But before long there were gusts and then a steady gale that howled and moaned and keened through the trees and around the eaves. Jane tried not to think about Jim Ludlow, who by now should be in Martinsburg or heading back with the oxygen tank and tent and a nurse.

She glanced down at the feverish little body in her arms. He was breathing raggedly and his temperature when she had checked it a bit ago had been up a tenth. She changed the baby's position.

"Let me have him now."

Although Mrs. Ludlow should be resting, Jane gave her the baby, and when the woman said, "They should be coming, shouldn't they?" shook her head. "It's too soon. In this storm."

"I suppose so."

In the kitchen, Jane found coffee, and the breakfast dishes undone. She dippered water from the reservoir of the huge range and washed them while the coffee perked.

"There's ham in the refrigerator," Amy Ludlow called from the bedroom.

Jane found it. And potato salad. She ate, and drank a cup of coffee.

"You'd better eat, too," she told Mrs. Ludlow. "And let's make more coffee. Your husband and the nurse will be chilled to the bone."

The woman raised frightened eyes from the baby. "He's—worse, don't you think?"

Was that a tinge, ever so faint, of blue on the little lips? Jane put down the stir of fear. A doctor doesn't panic—

CHAPTER 9

The hour plodded by, and if there was any lessening of the storm or a change for the better in the baby's labored breathing, neither Dr. Jane nor Amy Ludlow could see it.

The snow was an opaque curtain that sometimes billowed and swayed and swooped as the wind snatched back a few veils so they could see the pump ten feet from the kitchen door. Then the snow would close in again, like chiffon curtains dropped by an unseen stage hand, and the walls of the tiny farmhouse again were the far horizons of their world.

Surreptitiously Jane glanced at her watch. After four. They should be coming, unless something had happened.

But an accident *mustn't* have happened! Her eyes went anxiously to the baby. If they didn't come soon, it would be too late.

"Doctor Jane—" Mrs. Ludlow was holding her breath, straining to hear. "They're coming—they're coming!"

Jane listened, and heard nothing but the wind assaulting the treetops and scratching at a loose shutter somewhere.

Then she did hear, but it was only a snatch of sound that might have been a motor—or the wind playing tricks with their desperate need. She hurried to the door, slipped outside to stand listening while the storm buffeted her.

Faintly, for the wind was flinging the sound away from her, she heard the sturdy surge of two hundred horses, in low. Then a Cyclops' eye glared pinkly through the storm, reddening as it crept onward—

Forgetful of the storm, Jane ran toward the police car.

"Doctor Jane! Is he—is he—" Jim Ludlow sprang out of the car, grasped her roughly by the shoulders.

"He is very bad, Mr. Ludlow."

But she doubted if he heard. The wind wrenched the words from her lips and flung them wildly into the gray void that was the snow-filled, early darkness.

Hours, each of which must have been a separate eternity to Jim and Amy Ludlow, had dragged by. The wind still drove the snow yowlingly before it, but the frenzied, untamed concerto seemed to have dropped an octave or two.

Still the crisis had not come, although the tiny lips no longer were the cyanotic hue they had been. Through the clear plastic of the oxygen tent, Dr. Jane watched the rise and fall of the tiny chest.

Inhale, exhale, inhale, exhale . . . much, much too rapidly. And shallow.

There was nothing, now, that she could do. Nothing but wait, and watch.

And pray—*Bill* . . . "No change," she looked up to say when Jim Ludlow halted his pacing again at the bedroom door.

How many times tonight had she repeated that? Or the same answer in different words.

Ludlow didn't speak. Just stood for agonizing moments looking at his son, as he did each time, before he disappeared, a not-quite-silent wraith whose every footfall whispered his torment.

Jane glanced at Miss Delman, but the nurse was intent on her patient. A good nurse, Miss Delman. And, according to the state policeman who had answered Dr. Winters' appeal, "game."

The storm *was* lessening. Sometimes, now, there was a whole minute between gusts, then the banshee shriek began again, as mad as ever. Jim Ludlow appeared in the doorway, got the same answer, stood, hopeless, and went away.

He's given up, Jane thought.

They had finally prevailed upon Amy Ludlow to lie down, but now she returned. After having *not* slept, Jane was sure, although she had been up most of the previous night. From somewhere the doctor summoned a smile.

"Is he—better?" Mrs. Ludlow asked.

There had been no change, Jane told her.

"Then he's worse and you're not telling me. He can't be no better and not be worse. He can't just *lie there!*"

Her voice rose toward hysteria, a clenched fist pressed against her lips to hold it back.

"Amy—" Her husband was there suddenly. "Darling—"

"He's going to die, Jim! Our baby's going to die!"

"No, Am—Oh, God!" Weather-browned cheek pressed against her hair, he held her close.

"And the prayer of faith shall save the sick—"

Bill's voice, gentle, reassuring, as it always was when he read his text. Wasn't it strange that she should hear it now? Jane thought.

"You'll want coffee."

Amy Ludlow had hold of herself now. With a lingering, longing look at her baby, she went out; a moment later her husband followed.

"I can use that coffee." Nurse Delman was briskly professional.

Jane nodded.

They had their coffee, great, steaming mugs of it, and settled down again to their vigil. Miss Delman gave the thermometer a shake, tucked it under the baby's tongue.

"One oh four point seven."

Jane's heart gave a hopeful, and surprised, lurch. One oh four point seven for *two readings in a row!*

"Will you tell them, please, Miss Delman? It's—something."

It was indeed "something." A straw to hang onto. Fragile, inconclusive, but a *hope*.

Amy Ludlow crept into her chair and huddled there, her eyes scarcely leaving her baby and then only to seek in the nurse's or Dr. Jane's face the answer to her dread.

In the kitchen, Jim Ludlow clattered stove lids and coal bucket as he built up the fire. Then he began roaming the house again, haunting the bedroom door and moving on, as if by keeping always on the go he could measure his misery and, somehow, cope with it.

"What is it now?" He was there again, standing in the doorway.

At an almost imperceptible nod from Dr. Jane, Miss Delman took the baby's temperature. "One oh four point nine."

Jim Ludlow's big hands clenched.

—point nine, Dr. Jane repeated to herself.

Climbing again in spite of everything they had done . . .

Some time later Jane realized the wind had dropped to a whisper, but when it had lessened she didn't know. She went to the window. If it no longer was snowing, there was good reason—all the snow in the heavens seemed to be out there, drifted against fences, trees, her car. For delicious moments she let her forehead rest against the cold pane.

"It's stopped snowing."

"Thank goodness for that!" Miss Delman said fervently.

If we could have gotten him to the hospital, would it have made a difference? For a long time now the question had been nagging at the back of Jane's mind. Should we have risked it? Mr. Ludlow made it through to Martinsburg. The police car managed to get here.

"Doctor," Miss Delman said with that quiet authority nurses have at such a time.

In a flash, Jane was at the baby's side.

Another spasmodic, shuddery gasp, one small fist unfurling, waving—

Mrs. Ludlow gave a strangled sob and then cried out, "Jim!" Jane didn't look at her. Nor at Miss Delman. Aware of a hot stinging in her eyes, she put out a hand to touch the burning little forehead, and held it there—to be sure.

It couldn't be! It couldn't—*but it was*. The baby's forehead was cool, the tiny pulses in his throat no longer running away—

"Delman, for God's sake," Paul said.

"Paul, please—"

"Okay, okay. But if I'm ever snowbound, I hope it's not with that hag." He drew her to him, kissed her long and lingeringly, and as hungrily as though he never expected to kiss her again.

But it was just a kiss. She was tired to her marrow, that was why, Jane told herself, and thought how stunned Paul would be to know that she was analyzing his kiss while his lips still claimed hers.

And she was irritated with him, just a little. Miss Delman was *not* a hag.

"Paul—"

He held her from him, his dark eyes probing hers. "You're angry."

"No, Paul. Just very tired."

"And wearing your halo very straight." The kiss brushed lightly across her cheek. "Run along home to bed, darling. We have a date for dinner, remember."

Seething, Jane watched him go into his own office, put on his smart gray fedora, shrug into the gray tweed topcoat, pick up the black alligator bag, and leave.

Paul Hamlin, I hate you!

Only she didn't, and the next time he took her in his arms—

"'Brothers, we are treadddding"—Granny Mason sang to the back of Lucy Gray's head— "'Where the saints have trod—'" What she would give to hear Bill Latham singin' that! Not that the preacher could sing, she thought. Goodness knew he couldn't. But he put his heart in it and that was what counted.

"'All one body we, One in hope and doctrine, One in chariteeeee."

He wasn't like Paul Hamlin, the preacher wasn't. Look at him, settin' up there with Dr. Jane, that good-lookin' head throwed back singin' as if—as if, Granny stumbled over the unchristian thought, that song meant somethin' to him!

Granny knew what Bill Latham would say to that. "'Judge not, that ye be not judged.'"

And like as not, he'd go on with it. "'For with what judgement ye judge, ye shall be judged; and with what measure ye mete, it shall be measured to you again. And why beholdest thou the mote that is in thy brother's eye, but considerest not the beam that is in thine own eye?' Granny, Granny," he would say, shaking his head.

That was all right for a preacher, Granny thought, not seein' somethin' that was plain as the nose on his face. But there was things a body could tell.

Lucy Gray had held onto the note as long as she could. The ministerial student who came every Sunday from the seminary in Central City to preach to them rose.

"Father, go with us," he began the benediction, and Granny, chastened, did not even steal a glance at Paul Hamlin.

It was one of those rare December days. The wind from the south was almost balmy, the sunshine a comfort to old bones, Granny had thought more than once during the sermon, when the sun came warmly through the stained-glass windows to touch her. It had been a good sermon, she guessed, not as good as the preacher's, of course, but passable. It was just that, today, she couldn't keep her mind on it. Granny pursed her lips at that.

She didn't believe in goin' to church to woolgather, and today she had. Dr. Jane, and Bill Latham—

And Dr. Hamlin.

Granny thought with a sigh, Why did it have to be him that come to Halesville?

"Granny," Sue Latham said against her ear as they went outside, "Granny, if Jane and Paul ask us to ride, you go ahead. I—I'm going to walk."

CALLING DOCTOR JANE 67

The old woman didn't look at her. She didn't have to. She'd had a good life, and a good man, but many's the time, and this was one of them, Granny Mason had decided she wouldn't be young again for anything in this world.

"Give me your arm, Sue," she said, as if she hadn't heard. "I'm a mite unsteady on these here steps."

She nodded to the Bateses and halfway down stopped to say to Min Dawson, "I noticed Claude Gray lookin' at that carpet. He ought to, him pres'dent of the board."

Mrs. Dawson sniffed. "You know when we'll get a new carpet, Melvina Mason. When Lucy Gray gets to be president of Ladies' Aid, that's when."

"Girls, girls." Paul Hamlin took an arm of each. "Come along; we'll drop you off."

"You go ahead, Min. I think I'll walk. I'll be all right, too," Granny bridled when Dr. Hamlin started to protest. "Sue'll be right with me. And we'll walk slow."

"Well—"

"Of course, Granny." Jane gave her hand a little squeeze. "We won't be late. You'll come, Mrs. Dawson?"

The Queen of Sheba, at least, Granny thought, watching Paul Hamlin settle Min Dawson in the cream-colored car. And Min lappin' it up like a kitten at warm milk— "Some women ain't got the sense of a goose that's been eatin' sour mash!"

"Why, Granny!" Sue Latham forgot that to Granny she was one of them and burst out laughing.

Cynthia Peters came home from the hospital that week, and Joe Hiram was ready to go back to begin the therapy Dr. Jane hoped would give him full use of his arm and hand. Or what was left of the hand.

Now, examining the forearm and the hand she and Dr. Laird had, almost literally, rebuilt, her heart twisted. Thumb, two fingers, those poor gnarled stumps—

"Think I've got a chance, Dr. Jane?"

The farmer stopped massaging the hand to look at her. "I think so."

With his good forefinger Joe Hiram traced a metacarpal they had reconstructed. "Feels numb."

"We'll give therapy a crack at that," Jane told him. "I've made an appointment for you with Mr. Manning."

She told him when, and Hiram nodded.

"Next time," he said, rising, "I'll bet I ask that cornpicker a by your leave."

"You do that."

She walked with him through the empty waiting room to the door, exchanging remarks about the unseasonably warm weather— "After that snowstorm, too!" She shook her head smilingly.

"Well, we can stand it. Ten-thirty?" he asked, corroborating the time of his appointment with the physical therapist.

Jane said that it was.

Paul had a patient, the last of the afternoon, apparently, unless someone else came in before five. She went into the small laboratory, thinking, Why couldn't Dr. Ed putter around in here? He could run a few tests for them, perhaps even do some of the research he'd never had time for when he was practicing.

Thinking that, she got out the culture she had been watching and slid it into the microscope.

The telephone rang twice before she remembered Paul's patient. Hastily she reached for the extension.

"—see him, all right," a voice was saying.

Jace Perry, Jane identified it as, and quietly replaced the phone.

After a while, she heard Paul saying goodbye to his patient. He came in.

"Doctor Koch, I presume?" He bent and kissed the nape of her neck.

Jane smiled at the odd-shaped bacilli on the slide. Whenever she was in there, she was "Doctor Koch," or "Pasteur," or "Laveran" to Paul.

She straightened. "Look, Paul."

"Some other time. That was Jace Perry, Jane. He wants me to run over—"

CHAPTER 10

She didn't like Dr. Jason Perry and so she had set herself up in judgment. That was it, Jane thought—and it was wrong.

Even though Jace wasn't exactly in good standing in the medical society, it was wrong. Why shouldn't he want Paul to look at a patient? Although why he didn't call Dr. O'Donnell or one of the other Martinsburg physicians into consultation she didn't understand.

Jane let her magazine drop to her lap. It must be that opposites attract, she thought, for Paul certainly wasn't anything like Jace Perry, thank goodness.

Leaning back, she closed her eyes. She should write to Bill and tell him. She must tell him soon.

The yawn crept up on her unawares and Granny Mason said, "Tired out, ain't you?"

"Ummmm."

Granny put aside her tatting. "I'm goin' to fix you some hot cocoa and you're goin' to bed."

Jane started to protest and then didn't. It was nice to have decisions made for her, for a change. Yawning again, she followed Granny into the kitchen.

"Sage," she said, wrinkling her nose at the delicious, pungent aroma. That meant, sausage for breakfast, for Granny always added a dash of the seasoning from the supply she grew every summer in the back yard.

Sage, thyme, marjoram, and goodness knew what else were in tiny jars in the cupboard and always some of their fragrance lingered in the kitchen. No wonder Bill said he missed Granny's kitchen more than he did a shower that wasn't an old gasoline drum set up on iron pipes. She would, too.

No, she wouldn't, she thought. Granny would stay with her—or rather, go with her, for they wouldn't live here, she and Paul.

Not in a house that held so many memories of Bill . . .

For a wonder, there were no emergency calls that night. Or if there had been, Clara Mae Oley had rung Paul, Jane thought next morning.

It was early, barely six. Stretching and curling up like a puppy luxuriating in a spot of sunshine, she lay watching the elm lace against the brightening sky.

This morning she would see Cynthia Peters and the Rayburn baby, who had whooping cough, and in the afternoon she would be alone in the office. It was Paul's day to go to Stewart.

Jace Perry, she thought, then. Oh well, Paul would tell her—

She sat on the side of the bed, fumbling her feet into

slippers. A woman, no doubt. Most of Jace Perry's patients were women.

No. She remembered then.

"—see him, all right," Jace had said. What had been in his voice? What that was different from his usual suave, urbane manner?

For heaven's sake, Jane Langford!

Laughing at herself, she pulled on the woolly white robe and went down the hall to the bathroom. Imagine imagining Jace Perry being *sinister!*

There was sausage for breakfast, huge country patties. And eggs for which Granny had sent Sue to the farm yesterday.

Granny was finding a lot of errands that needed running to the farm these days, Jane thought and wondered if Sue suspected. She glanced at the girl. But Sue was intent on the morning paper, with Bill's frown puzzling her brows.

She must hate me, Jane thought. Because of both Paul and Bill—

" 'Sing, choirs of an-gels, Sing in ex-ul-ta-tion—' Now, then," Bill Latham said, "let's try it together. 'Sing, choirs of an-gels, Sing in—' "

They followed him perfectly, as they had through every note of Luther's *Cradle Hymn* and "Joy to the World," learning a line at a time, with him reading it first and then singing it for them. "All together now—" He felt like one of those pioneer circuit riders lining a hymn for a congregation that pretty soon would have the rafters—or the brush arbors—ringing.

" 'Sing, all ye ci-tiz-ens Of heav'n a-bove—" He recited the next line and then sang it, careful to observe all the "breaks" and "holds." A baker's dozen young voices echoed, and when they came to the chorus it seemed the thatched roof should take joyous wing.

" 'O come, let us adore Him, O come, let us adore Him, O come, let us adore Him, Christ the Lord.' "

"Good, good," he applauded, and suddenly was aware that another pair of hands was clapping in time to his own. "What do you think of my choir, Al?"

The missionary doctor came forward grinning. "Never heard better."

"Nor have I. That's all for now, kids." And when they had gone scampering, "It's too bad they've got to have a guy like me for a song leader, though. How's that tenor of yours?"

"Worse than yours." Al Donaldson laughed.

"Could it be?"

Donaldson took off his pith helmet and mopped sweat. "Christmas," he said. "Snowball fights. Ice skating. Taffy pulls."

"You're homesick."

"The only time of year it gets me." The doctor put his helmet back on as they walked out into the blinding sun. "Not exactly homesickness, Bill. Nostalgia, maybe—a remembering."

Bill knew, and he nodded. It wouldn't be homesickness; Africa had been home to Al Donaldson for almost twenty years, would be for twenty more or however long he lived. But memories and yearnings for the bright dreams — He said quickly, "Asey-for-short said you would bring cloth for the costumes."

"I brought it. You turning wardrobe mistress, too?"

"That's Keaa's job. And Asey's, although I'm a little 'juberous' of the combination."

"I thought Asey was back on the straight and narrow."

"Oh, he is. But—"

"I know. 'But.'" Dr. Donaldson whumped him heartily on the back. "Come on, boy, let's unload."

As usual, the Jeep was loaded to the gunnels with supplies and mail, and by the time they had finished unloading both men were more than ready for the cooling drink Asey-for-short had waiting. If he let himself, Bill had often thought, he could be suspicious of Asey's concoctions, but he was reasonably sure there was no copper tubing rigged up for distillation, and besides, Asey hadn't backslid for a long time. It had been at least four months . . . well, almost.

"Another?" he asked Al.

"Don't care if I do."

It was a ritual. Asey-for-short would be crushed if they didn't refill their glasses. And he would know. He might be across the compound showing the kids how he played mumblety-peg, but he would know, Bill thought.

Donaldson drained his glass of the fruity mixture and brought out his pipe. This was the time of the doctor's visits Bill had come to look forward to. They discussed Africa, the state of the world, themselves, and ideologies and the philosophies they lived by, and sometimes Bill found himself feeling sorry for the big man who now sat scrunched down in the reed chair. It was going to be such a long time before Africa achieved the good things he visualized for her.

"There's encephalitis downriver."

"Much?"

"Half a dozen cases. Probably more—who knows?"

Who knew indeed? Isolated cases about whom word didn't seep through until too late.

"Those damned flies," Donaldson said, and didn't apologize.

Bill knew how he felt, frustrated, helpless. He felt the same way when he preached to impassive, veiled eyes and had the sick, empty feeling that he wasn't getting across to them the truth that his Saviour was their Saviour, who cared. Then the mask would crumble, on only one ebony face, perhaps, and Browning would be right again, "God's in His heaven: All's right with the world."

"You know the symptoms?"

"Drowsy, and I think I read somewhere, headachy. I suppose you'd better brief me."

Donaldson would, he promised, but later. Now he had better get busy, and he hoped he didn't find any runny noses and fever—

Encephalitis symptoms, Bill decided, watching the big man shoulder aside the sunshine as he went outside. Well, forewarned was forearmed. At least he could keep a sharp eye out for the symptoms. And do what? Send Asey-for-short to fetch Al, who couldn't be spared?

With a sigh, he crossed the room to the desk on which he had tossed the mail. A letter from Sue, a brief note from Jane, which he'd already opened. Settling down at the desk, he began Sue's letter and stopped. That was funny. She'd never mentioned wanting to come out here before. He read on, but that was all.

Just "Could we afford for me to come to Africa?"

Not *too* or *come with Jane*—

Without actually being aware of the motions, he folded the letter and tucked it into its envelope. "Could we afford for me to come to Africa?"

There was other mail. The bundle of Sunday-school literature, papers and colored picture cards. A denominational paper. The magazines to which he subscribed, and the Martinsburg newspapers which somehow found their way halfway round the world. He pushed them aside to devour at his leisure and slit open an envelope bearing a Halesville postmark.

From Granny, probably, he was thinking when he saw that it wasn't.

Dear Brother Latham, it read.

The Bible says "take heed that your heart be not deceived—"

December was slipping by. Sue had gone to her aunt's in Memphis and would not return until after New Year's, and the big old house seemed strangely empty without her.

And for the first time since that first year after her father died, Jane found herself actually dreading Christmas. Dr. Ed had invited them, Granny, Paul and her. And the Old Doctor had a way of picking her thoughts as if they were bones lying bare on a desert somewhere.

He might not mention Bill, he seldom did these days, but Bill would be in his thoughts.

No, not a suit. Not tonight when she needed to feel festive . . . She hung it back, selected the gold crepe. It brought a hint of tawniness to her magnolia-cream skin, a new warmth to her hazel eyes, the salesgirl in Central City had told her.

Inspecting her reflection in the long mirror, Jane couldn't see the change, but no matter. The dress was just about perfect and tonight she wouldn't be Jane Langford, M. D. She would be Jane Langford who one day soon was going to marry Paul—

The thought sent a tiny quiver of excitement coursing through her. Mrs. Paul Hamlin.

But still Dr. Jane Langford, professionally . . .

She was waiting when Paul came.

"Good evening, darling."

"Jane." He kissed her, but his lips found a pulse in her throat, not her lips. "There ought to be a law against you," he said huskily. He put her from him then. "Ready?"

Her nod was shaky.

"What shall we tell Mrs. Mason? The Martin House?"

"Not—not the Martin House, Paul."

For heaven's sake, why not? something within her cried. Bill hasn't got a priority on Johnny's and Tina's steaks.

"The Country Club, then?" he suggested.

She nodded and went to tell Granny.

The Country Club was all dressed up for the holidays. A tree, so tall its star brushed the ceiling, gay baubles, tinsel, candles—on the tree and banked in the windows and on the tables—carols so soft they were background only.

"Oh, Paul, it's beautiful!" Jane breathed as they paused in the doorway.

"Then you belong in it."

He guided her to a table and at once the waiter was there.

"Steak," Jane told Paul. "Well done."

"Not tonight, darling. We're celebrating. I don't know what, but we are. Pheasant," he said to the waiter, "with that chestnut dressing. You take it from there."

Across the room Dr. Jancieski, the radiologist at the Martinsburg hospital, raised a hand in greeting. His pretty wife smiled.

"Isn't Mrs. Jancieski stunning?" Jane said.

"If you like ash-blondes."

Jane laughed. "Goodness, don't you?"

Paul's hands came across the table to cover hers. "You know what I like, my darling. A certain very special hazel-eyed brunette with a wide ready smile that does as much for her patients as the medicine she prescribes." The hands on hers tightened. "I mean that, Jane."

The dark eyes claimed hers and held them, and the world around them ceased to exist. There was only the wavering candle flame and—Paul.

CHAPTER 11

The market place was gay, and overflowing as it always was with produce, souvenirs, that particular babel that goes with market days, and small boys. Jane would love it, Bill Latham thought and then caught himself up.

He was going to have to stop telling himself Jane this and Jane that—he was going to have to stop *thinking* about her. It was over. Ended. It didn't matter that Jane hadn't told him herself—well, he supposed she *had*, in a way. Her letters were brief lines, with volumes between those lines.

Wishing that he knew what sort of guy this Paul Hamlin

was, he moved on, pausing now and then to bargain for a piece of cloth, a silver trinket, one of the brilliantly printed pagnes the women wore. He already had gifts for the children, and the Ladies' Aid in Halesville had sent him hard candy which had arrived all gooey from the heat. With these presents for Keaa and Asey-for-short, who were his right hands, and a pipe for Al Donaldson, he was all set.

And had better get going, he reminded himself. Driving through those papyrus swamps in the dark, even in the Jeep, would be no picnic.

He wasn't sure why he had come to Kampala, anyway. Because it was a long, hard drive, he supposed, and would leave him too bone-tired to think.

Only it hadn't. Jane was everywhere, haunting his dreams, taunting him in every waking moment. They had been so sure of their love, he and Jane.

He still was. Of *his*. If he lived to Methuselah's nine hundred and sixty-nine years, he would still be sure . . .

Asey-for-short, which Bill called him because he couldn't begin to wrap his tongue around the man's native name, was waving from the porch when he drove up. Kampala was a blown manifold gasket and nearly three days behind, and the little mission station looked as Bill in this moment imagined Heaven would look.

And sounded the way Heaven would sound. From somewhere Keaa's clear soprano was singing, "Sun, moon and stars forgot, Upward I fly, Still all my song shall be, Nearer, my God, to Thee, Nearer, my God, to Thee . . . Nearer, to Thee."

He returned Asey-for-short's grin.

"All five verses, Mist' Latham." Asey reached for bundles. "You have good trip."

"I guess so, Asey. Kampala's quite a town."

"Yessuh."

Asey had been all over. All the way to Lagos, he had boasted once. He knew every water hole and native village and had his own uncanny way of keeping in touch. Bill didn't know how he did it and wasn't sure he wanted to know, and he wasn't superstitious, either, he sometimes argued with Al Donaldson.

The shank of the day in which he had arrived home was gone before he knew it. Night came down all at once, as it seemed to do in the tropics, and beyond the circle of light cast by the gasoline lantern was thick, velvety blackness but not silence. The hum of myriad insects, the deep bass roar of a bull crocodile down by the river, from somewhere a native chant, not weird now as it had been when he first came—

Beyond the woven-reed partition, Asey-for-short was settling down for the night, or preparing to slip out into the night— Bill Latham wasn't sure which. With Asey, you never knew. Just that he would be there come dawn, the same old bouncing-with-energy Asey, as eager to please as always.

He began reading where the Book fell open. "In Thee, O Lord, do I put my trust; let me never be put to confusion. Deliver me into Thy righteousness, and cause me to escape; incline Thine ear unto me—"

"Mist' Latham!"

Asey had materialized at his side, was clutching his arm. "Mist' Latham, that croc he get boy!"

He heard the screaming then. Terrified shrieks that must come from a score of throats, wails, lamentations—

Incline Thine ear unto us, Lord, Bill Latham prayed as he leaped for the door. Those kids knew better than to— He didn't finish the thought. The compound was deserted, the blackness beyond it lightning-bugged with torches, lanterns, flashlights. Springing back to grab his own lantern, he ran for them.

"Mist' Bill!" Keaa flung herself upon him. "Oh oh oh ohhhh—"

"Get hold of yourself, Keaa!"

Giving her a shake, he pushed through the tight little circle to where the boy lay on the ground, writhing, screaming, bleeding horribly. But the leg was still there.

"Easy, fella."

Bill dropped to one knee, peeling off his shirt as he did so. A tourniquet—and then Al Donaldson? Someone would have to go. Asey, he supposed. Asey handled the Jeep as if it were part of him: Asey would never have spent hours struggling with a manifold gasket . . .

Strange, Bill Latham was to think later, the thoughts that run through a guy's head, sometimes. That confounded gasket, the herd of elephants that had descended on the water hole the other evening just after he'd cleared out fast, day after tomorrow, Christmas, which suddenly had lost its glow— And all the time he was talking to the boy, ministering to him the best he could, and finally giving him a shot of the Demerol Al had left to ease his pain and terror.

He hadn't known a night could be so long. The tourniquet had to be loosened frequently, and whenever it was, the bleeding began again. Bill supposed that indicated an artery or a vein had been torn and if Asey didn't hurry—

Which was so foolish it was ludicrous. By now that Jeep would have sprouted wings and a propeller in sheer self-defense, but even so there were many torturous miles and if Al wasn't at Carter's station— A whimpering moan from the cot put the fear from him.

The kid was coming around again.

"Keaa!" Bill called.

"Come look at our tree, Dr. Jane!"

Cynthia Peters' eyes were dancing, and before long her feet would be, too. Her incision was healing beautifully.

"Sugared popcorn," she said, pointing to the fluffy white balls and stars and even angels that were hanging on the Scotch pine. "One of the nurses' aides at the hospital told me how her grandmother used to make them for her and her brothers and sisters."

"So nothing would do," Mrs. Peters chimed in, "but Cynthy and Tommy had to make them. The kitchen was a mess."

"It always is when I cook, too," Jane said. She went to the tree, touched one of the balls, and licked her fingers. "I'll bet you eat them."

"Oh, yes. That's part of the fun, nibbling angels." Cynthia giggled.

Jane laughed, too. It was so good to hear merriment bubbling from the girl's lips, and to see color in her face. And she'd bet Mrs. Peters didn't mind a bit having her kitchen "a mess."

Carefully Cynthia took down one of the popcorn stars and handed it to Jane. "It's really the Star over Bethlehem. I told Tommy when we were making them I wished you could have one." The blue eyes were shining. "I've so much to be thankful for, Dr. Jane."

She could have howled, Jane told Dr. O'Donnell later when she met him in one of the corridors at the hospital in Martinsburg.

"I know," he nodded.

"I don't know whether it was her faith, or the Star, or a whole combination of things," Jane had been trying to figure it out ever since, "but I had my Christmas right then. I'm afraid tomorrow is going to be anticlimax."

Dr. O'Donnell gave her a long, steady look. "There are some things, Jane, that even we can't analyze."

"Yes."

How many times had they both, and every other doctor, seen it? The patient who by Faith alone lived when they didn't see how he could and the patient who should have gone on living—and didn't. Because he had lost that Touch . . .

A smile curved Jane's lips. "I guess you might say Cynthia was good for me."

"It may be platitudinous, but a successfully convalescent patient is good for all of us. Which way're you headed? I'm bound for the lab."

"O. b.," Jane told him, and a few minutes later was riding up to Second Floor, West.

The rest of the day was slow. Afternoon office hours were practically empty. As Paul dryly observed, nobody wanted to be "poked and probed and diagnosed" on Christmas Eve.

"We might as well close up early," he suggested.

"You go along. I think I'll stay."

"And get tied up at five minutes until five with Lord knows what." Hands jammed in his pockets, he stood at the window. "It's starting to rain."

Apprehension prickled along Jane's spine. Rain, freezing rain, and Christmas Eve.

"I believe I will, darling." He kissed her. "Sure you won't change your mind?"

"Absolutely."

When he had gone, she puttered. There was nothing else to do. No case histories to be brought up to date and filed. No tests to run; there had been no patients who needed a blood count or a throat culture. No wonder Paul found Halesville dull sometimes, she thought. He wasn't accustomed to these periods of delightful nothingness.

She was deep in an article on heart surgery when someone entered the waiting room. She rose, went to the door of her office.

"Good afternoon. Could I—"

"Hamlin!" the man said. "Where's Doc Hamlin?"

"He has gone for the afternoon."

The man stared at her unbelievingly.

"I'm Dr. Langford. Perhaps I—"

He shook his head, muttered somehing about "seein' the doc later," and all but bolted.

Well, Jane thought.

Frowning, but only a little, she went to the door. In the gathering dark a motor raced, and then the dark shape that was a car went hurtling past. For heaven's sake, he was upset!

It was almost five and when it was, she locked the doors and drove the block home. The first floor was aglow. Granny liked lights. "It takes lamps, lots of 'em, to make a house beautiful," she declared, and Jane thought now, Our house is. From the street you could see the shelves of books that climbed to the ceiling on either side of the fireplace, and in the dining room the old hanging lamp would be glistening in every prism and touching fingers of light to the polished walnut paneling.

The rain was pelting down now, but at least it wasn't freezing. It would, though, she thought as she hurried inside. The temperature was too borderline.

Paul would say she was borrowing trouble. Well, perhaps she was. But tonight was Christmas Eve and— "Merry Christmas, Granny darling!" Jane kissed her.

"Where's Dr. Hamlin? Ain't he comin'?"

Jane shook her head. "Not until later. He's going to the church with us, though."

And later they were going to the Country Club Christmas party, but she didn't tell Granny that. Granny wouldn't approve.

She sniffed. "Granny! You've got plum pudding!"

"Turkey, too. One of them little ones. And oyster dressin' and cramberries. I—I figger Christmas is for fam'lies, Dr. Jane, and—and—"

"Granny," Jane whispered past the tight, hot lump that suddenly was in her throat.

She was upstairs, dressing, when she heard Paul's knock. The black velvet suit with its stunningly simple eggshell satin blouse was demure enough for church and sophisticated enough for the party. Paul would adore it, she thought as she fastened the tiny amethyst earrings he had given her. There!

One last pirouette to inspect stocking seams and she was ready . . .

"Darling!"

Paul rose from the cherry-red wing chair and came to take her in his arms. "I hope you took a good look at yourself?"

"I did."

"Then you can't blame me." His lips touched hers, lightly at first and then crushingly.

A mighty pulse thundered in her ears, her heart somersaulted and lay trembling. Paul—oh Paul, Paul!

"Jane," he murmured finally against her lips, "Jane—"

She thought he was going to kiss her again, but instead he cupped her chin between thumb and forefinger and said soberly, "There'll be no more of that, Dr. Langford."

"Doctor's orders?"

"Doctor's orders." He grinned. "Run fix your mouth, sweetheart."

The church was nearly full. They found seats down front on the side, and Jane sat listening to the rustle of voices and skirts and children's excitement. There would be a treat and gifts from the tree, the program of recitations and songs, and Mr. Gray would read the Christmas story which Granny said Mrs. Gray said he had been practicing reading aloud for days.

Jane smiled at the thought. He probably would do better if he simply got up and began reading. Now he would be petrified and might even stutter, as he did sometimes under stress.

The choir came in singing. "O come, all ye faithful, Joyful and triumphant," and at a signal from Miss Riley, the high-school music teacher who was directing this year, the congregation joined in, "O come ye, O come ye To Bethlehem—"

Beside her, Paul's voice rang out loud and true and on the other side Granny was singing her sweet heart out.

"I—I figger Christmas is for fam'lies—"

Impulsively Jane reached over and squeezed the bony, blue-veined hand.

The opening hymn finished, the recitations and songs began, some of them quavery as much with anticipation as stage fright, Jane decided when more than one pair of eyes darted to the tree and had trouble disentangling themselves from the presents heaped about it on the floor.

Bill would have his cantata tomorrow—today, the thought corrected itself, for already it was Christmas Day there— She bit her lip. She hadn't intended thinking about Bill tonight.

Purposefully she fastened her attention on Larry Burton's young nephew, who was valiantly reciting, "Christmas bells are sounding clear, Over church and dwelling—" He was a lot like Larry, and probably Larry at nine had been just as bashful and determined not to show it.

CALLING DOCTOR JANE

Was it still raining? she wondered. And getting colder? She had thought so when they came, but the church, packed so full, was stifling. Why didn't someone open a window?

She had forgotten to tell Paul about the man, Jane remembered after a time and the reason she had forgotten burned her face. If Paul could do that to her, she must be right—oh, she must be!

"*Adeste, fideles, Laeti triumphantes*," Miss Riley was singing softly, reverently, in Latin, "*Venite, venite—*"

"Somebody's killed Mr. Bates!"

Miss Riley stopped singing, a stunned look on her face.

The boy cried out, "The door's open and—come quick!"

CHAPTER 12

Mr. Bates was crumpled just inside the door of the back room in which he compounded prescriptions, and Ron Delafield was right: The back door, which opened into the alley opposite the vacant parsonage garden, stood open.

"He left that way," someone said.

There was a rumble of agreement, but Dr. Jane, on her knees beside the old druggist, scarcely heard. Gentle fingers were exploring the ugly head wound, seeking a pulse and finding it frighteningly weak.

"I'll phone for an ambulance." Paul got to his feet. "Don't touch anything, anybody." His voice rose. "There may be fingerprints. And keep back, give him air."

The whole congregation had stampeded to the drugstore and already had done goodness knew how much to impede any investigation. But Jane thought of that only fleetingly. The injury was a dangerous one and Mr. Bates wasn't young.

"Money's in the cash register all right," a voice said.

And another, "The kid musta scared him off."

"Yeah. Lucky he didn't get his head busted, too."

"What in tunket's going on in here?"

The Old Doctor's voice blasted a path for him. And when he saw, "For God's sake."

Jane gave him a swift, worried glance.

"What happened?" the Old Doctor demanded.

"Don't know," Claude Gray told him. "The Delafield boy

found him. He was going along the alley and noticed the door was open. He yelled in, 'Your door's open, Mr. Bates. Want me to close it?' and when nobody answered, he came on in."

"For God's sake," Dr. Ed echoed himself. He knelt beside Jane, and tender fingers touched his friend's head. "Bad, isn't it, Janie?"

Jane nodded.

"An ambulance is on the way." Paul came pushing through the group. "I called State Police and the sheriff's office, too." He went to take both Mrs. Bates's hands in his. "Mrs. Bates, come sit down."

She shook her head.

"Who would do such a thing, Dr. Hamlin?" she moaned. "Who?"

"I don't know, Mrs. Bates," he said gently.

"If he had just taken the money—" Mrs. Bates broke off and buried her face in her hands.

Paul gave her shoulder a consoling pat. He looked around. "Where's that boy? What's his name? Delafield?"

"Here, sir."

"Oh. Yes." For a long minute Paul stood looking down at Mr. Bates. Then, "You didn't hear—anything, Delafield? What's your first name again?"

Ron told him. And, "No, sir. I didn't hear a sound."

"See anybody, meet anyone while you were walking through the alley?"

"No, sir. I guess just about everybody was at the church."

Paul sighed. "I guess they were. What time did Mr. Bates plan to close up? After all, it's—"

Christmas Eve, Jane finished silently.

"Anybody know?" he asked the uncomfortable silence.

"Seven-thirty," Mrs. Bates sobbed. "He let Betty off early and was going to keep open till seven-thirty and meet me at the church. I th-thought he was back in the crowd some—" She couldn't finish.

From outside, and rapidly loudening, came the angry wail of a siren.

Christmas was a nightmare. Despite long hours in Surgery, Mr. Bates lay unconscious, seeming sometimes scarcely to breathe. Jane hadn't left him.

"Any change?"

Dr. Laird came in again, his lean, earnest face showing few

signs that he had been in the operating room most of the night.

She shook her head.

The surgeon studied the bottle of dextrose and water. "Hadn't you better get some rest?"

"Mr. Bates was a good friend to me. I used to jerk sodas for him." Her eyes went to the bloodless face, white as the pillow. "I'll stay."

Dr. Laird nodded.

"Blood pressure?"

"One ten over seventy."

"Still holding that, eh? Good."

He went out, to look in on other patients, and Jane settled down to her vigil. She had borrowed a pair of Oxfords from one of the students—they looked oddly out of place with the black velvet suit, but those black velvet pumps would have been worse than useless in the operating room.

Closing her eyes, she re-lived those hours. Four hours of exhausting surgery to try to relieve the pressure X-rays had shown existed.

And now dicoumeral for the clot that already had developed before they operated. A not-too-massive clot. The dicoumeral should do it—

Yawning, Jane rose. She would ask Mrs. Young for another cup of coffee.

The afternoon dragged into evening. Christmas, Jane thought, and this. Mrs. Bates had returned and was holding her husband's hand, stroking it, sometimes saying, "Charley? Can you hear me, Charley?"

There was no response, no break in the steady, shallow breathing, not the flicker of a muscle.

The Bateses' daughter motioned Dr. Jane into the hall. "Shouldn't there be a change soon?"

"Yes. Soon."

"He's going to die, isn't he?"

Jane met her eyes. "I don't know. We're doing all we can."

They were, but was it enough? Jane was beginning to be terribly afraid that it wasn't. Mrs. Harper was right. There should be a change soon, and she was afraid—afraid—

Who? she thought. Who?

Mr. Bates never hurt anybody, and if someone didn't have the money for a prescription or a bottle of the patent medicine on his shelves—well, they didn't need to worry about that, either.

Conjecture was running wild, Paul had said when he dropped in. The Delafield boy wasn't lily-white. He had a girl and girls can be expensive, and when you've just got an after-school and Saturday job sweeping out a grocery—

Jane couldn't believe that. Ron Delafield wouldn't.

But somebody had, and until Mr. Bates regained consciousness they wouldn't know. Even in her own mind, she refused to say "unless Mr. Bates regained consciousness."

The *Martinsburg Sun* had a field day.

DRUGGIST ATTACKED IN CHRISTMAS EVE MYSTERY

the headline screamed.

Jane scanned the story, but there was nothing new. She folded the paper, laid it beside her plate.

"Going back to the hospital?" the Old Doctor asked.

"Don't worry about me, Dr. Ed. I'm all right."

She was. Weariness no longer washed over her in waves as it had after nearly forty-eight scarcely interrupted hours at Mr. Bates's bedside.

"Of course you are."

Dr. Ed, who had come across to have breakfast with her, chewed on the cigar he no longer lighted. "What do you make of it, Janie?"

Attempted robbery, the paper said. The holdup man frightened off. It must have been that way.

He would have asked for something and then followed Mr. Bates into the back room. And then panicked and fled out the back door? But that was what Paul said people were saying about Ronnie Delafield—

"I don't know. Paul says there's talk about Ron Delafield."

"I've heard it. And I don't believe it!"

The Old Doctor bit down hard on his cigar. "I brought that boy into the world—" He broke off, shaking his head. "I know, I know. That's not proof of anything. But I've seen the boy grow up, Janie."

Rising, Jane patted his hand. "I know. I don't believe it, either."

"Going now?"

She nodded.

Paul's car was not in its usual parking place in front of their office, so she drove on, out Main Street past the drugstore and Smith's Grocery where Ron Delafield worked. It was the most natural thing in the world for Ron to cut through the alley on his way home; he probably did it every evening. And when he saw the drugstore door open he had done what anyone else would have done, called to Mr. Bates.

"Step lively now," the young Air Force man who had wanted to pay for her coffee in Louisville said with a grin. "This is a real whistle stop. By the time you stop hearing the whistle, the train's gone again."

Sue Latham managed a wisp of a smile.

"Halesville! Next stop . . . Halesville," the conductor's words came floating ahead of him.

"I'm sorry. I shouldn't try to jolly you up." The blue eyes were solemn now, sympathetic. "I hope you find the old man better."

She wouldn't. She knew she wouldn't. That AP story said "critical" and—

"Thank you."

"You're getting off at Halesville, Miss?"

Sue said she was and followed the conductor along the aisle. No one would meet her, she hadn't even wired Granny, but the one small bag that was all she had taken time to pack wasn't heavy. Aunt Tacey would send the rest of her things.

The airman—"First Class, but just," he had told her proudly, pointing to his brand-new stripe—was right. She barely had time to get both feet on the ground before the train pulled out. No wonder Granny said Halesville wasn't "a gnat in the railroad's eye" except for the freight cars that backed up on the spur that ran in to Clay Morton's factory.

Thinking that, she started walking.

"You hear about Charley Bates, Miss Latham?" the station agent wanted to know.

Sue nodded. "How—how is he?"

The man swallowed his Adam's apple. "You ain't *heard*?"

"He's—d-dead?"

"Couple hours ago. I hear they're arresting Joe Delafield's boy."

A week after the funeral Halesville was still up in arms. And divided into two camps: Ron Delafield did and Ron Delafield didn't.

There were points to be made on both sides and, as Paul pointed out, circumstantial evidence could be damning. And circumstantial evidence there was. Jane had to admit that. Henry Smith didn't know for sure what time Ron left the store. He'd told the kid he could go as soon as he finished up in the back, and sometimes Ron was a fast worker and sometimes he—well, he fiddled around. He had been busy with a late customer—who, everybody knew, was Sam Christy and his pinochle board.

"Christy's no better," Paul said. "Sit him down at a pinochle board and you could blow up the town."

"I know. But, Paul, we've go to do something."

"What? The police are doing all they can, darling. It's just one of those things. The guy got scared off."

"But it's murder, Paul."

"But not premeditated. That'll be one thing in Delafield's favor."

"Paul—"

"Look, Jane—let's be realistic. The kid had the opportunity, even the motive. Money. He slipped in that back door, conked Bates, and then lost his nerve when he realized he was going to have to walk through that brightly lighted front room to the cash register."

Her lips tightening, Jane turned back to the window, through which, somehow, Halesville didn't seem the same at all. Paul was right. The police were doing everything possible. Even with Ronnie Delafield in jail, they weren't letting up.

Did that mean they weren't satisfied, either?

"Paul," she said after a time, "suppose everybody is on the wrong tack. Suppose it wasn't money at all."

She knew what he was thinking, that they, she, Paul, and Dr. Ed, had checked the drug supplies and found nothing missing. She went on, slowly, feeling her way, "We could call the pharmaceutical houses Mr. Bates did business with, find out just what he had bought lately and how much. And then check the prescription files against the amounts in the drugstore now."

Paul shook his head. "An addict would have cleaned out the place. Killed someone else if he had to, but he wouldn't have left empty-handed."

"That's just it, Paul. How can we be sure he did?"

They couldn't, Paul agreed. Not if Mr. Bates had just gotten in an order. But what hophead would be thinking straight enough to leave some to allay suspicion?

Jane couldn't answer that one. It *didn't* run true to form, but narcotics twisted minds, made them diabolically clever sometimes.

Suppose one of those desperate creatures had found Mr. Bates alone in the drugstore? Had tried to buy a—a *jolt*, didn't they call it?

"It's a needle in a haystack, darling," Paul said after a time, "and I don't mind saying I think we're wasting our time—but let's give it a try, shall we?"

He reached for the ringing telephone. "Dr. Hamlin speaking."

Jane listened without listening. Paul was indulging her, and when she was proved wrong he would refrain from saying, "I told you so!" But what if she were right?

Ron Delafield wasn't an addict or about to become one, so it would have to be someone else.

Some transient, perhaps, caught far from his supply—

Her heart stopped beating and then gave a frightened leap. That man! The one who had come asking for Paul!

With her eyes wide open, she could see the nervous, jumpy movements, the strange eyes. For heaven's sake, how could she *not* have suspected?

She wasn't even sure that she had remembered to tell Paul at all, for that night when she had thought of it they had been in church and then Mr. Bates—

"Sounds like chickenpox," Paul said, hanging up. "One of the Jacoby children."

"Paul—"

"Darling, what's the matter? I said chickenpox, not leprosy."

"Paul," she began again . . .

"Jane!" when she had told him. "You don't—you *can't* think I—" The enormity of it struck him again. "Good lord!"

She didn't think that, no matter how it sounded.

"He—might have thought a prescription—"

"Which I would have written for him?"

"I didn't say that, Paul." She put both hands to his face, drew it down to hers.

She kissed him. "I said 'might have thought,' darling. A dope addict is a desperate, dangerous person."

"What did he look like?"

Jane described him. Thin, tall—six feet, maybe, wearing

an ill-fitting dark suit . . . "Blue, I'm almost sure." But it was his eyes she remembered best. Wild, shifty, *intense*.

The frown kept plucking at Paul's brows.

"The police aren't going to like it, Jane. Your forgetting, I mean."

"I know. I shouldn't have."

Paul jammed hands in his pocket and stood staring at the floor. "They're going to ask questions, Jane, some un-nice questions."

Yes, Jane thought. They would. How could she have forgotten? Why hadn't she told them sooner?

"I—know."

"I wonder if you do." He took her by the shoulders. "A policeman's mind, Jane, runs to suspicion. It's his business, just as medicine is yours and mine. His first thought is going to be that by waiting you have been protecting yourself—or me."

"But, Paul, I haven't!"

"I know that, darling." He drew her into his arms. "But don't expect the police to believe you."

CHAPTER 13

Lieutenant Jefferson held the pencil by its eraser and pushed it absently, making wiggly lines on the back of an envelope.

"Probably," he said after a time, "he was just somebody who didn't want to tell his troubles to a woman doctor. But there's always a chance."

There was, Jane thought. A darn good chance. If he and Paul could have seen the man—

Jefferson turned to Paul. "You say he didn't find you?"

"That's right."

The officer thought about that for a moment. "He could have consulted someone else. In Martinsburg, say. It shouldn't be too difficult to check, being Christmas Eve and all."

Jane winced.

"Nothing personal, Dr. Jane." Lieutenant Jefferson shook his head at her. "Don't feel too bad about it. You doctors are pretty good psychiatrists, too; you know how shock can set up a mental block."

It could, of course it could!

But that didn't excuse her. If she had telephoned Paul in the first place—

Asey-for-short was grinning all over his handsome black face.

"Mist' Caldwell, he come."

"Swell!" Bill Latham jumped up. "Thanks, Asey." And when he reached the door and saw no one, not even a cloud of dust that announced the approach of a vehicle, "Where is he?"

"Two, three hour," Asey-for-short said confidently. "He come."

Bill didn't see how they did it. Drums, he often thought, although he hadn't heard any. For all he knew it could be mental telepathy, but one thing he did know: a little before dark the missionary would arrive.

And, coming so late, he would spend the night. Bill grinned. "We've work to do, Asey."

"You betcha."

Asey-for-short had picked up his English in divers places, Bill gathered. Sometimes, when dealing with recalcitrant natives, it was pretty salty for a missionary's factotum, but Bill didn't know what he would do without him. Now Asey-for-short set to with a will. It was in one of "Mist'" Caldwell's services that he had been converted and, Bill Latham thought once with a silent chuckle, you would have thought royalty was coming visiting.

By the time the missionary arrived, and it was just as night was gathering to drop, all at once, like a blue-purple mist, the little mission station was ready. Twisted hanks of grasses and lengths of wood were ready to kindle a fire around which the natives would sing hymns and listen to Dr. Caldwell preach, and inside the square, thatched building that was Bill's quarters, Asey-for-short had supper ready.

"Well, Bill—"

Thin, wiry Barker Caldwell got out of the Jeep as though he hadn't driven all day. "It's good to see you. And you, Asey." He shook hands with both men. "Asey, I see you're taking good care of Reverend Latham."

Asey-for-short grinned all over. "You betcha. You want suppa now?"

Later, when they had eaten and the natives had sung and

Dr. Caldwell had spoken to them, the two missionaries sat for a long time talking . . . Beyond the glow from the gasoline lantern the night was a piece of black velvet, seemingly as thick and as soft. There were sounds, but they were soft sounds, gentle sounds—a shred of native tongue riding an errant, hot zephyr, a footfall—man or beast? Bill used to wonder, although now he accepted their comings and goings. Tonight no bull crocodile bellowed, though, no shrieks rent the dark—

Bill Latham shuddered. Would he never forget? The boy, Keaa's young nephew, wouldn't, he'd wager, he was thinking when Barker Caldwell broke one of their companionable silences.

"Are you happier now, Bill?"

"How did you know I wasn't?"

The smile that Bill had seen in the pulpit, in Martinsburg and here in Africa where Barker Caldwell's pulpit was wherever he happened to be, touched the older man's face.

"It was written all over you. I was beginning to be afraid you regretted coming."

Bill shook his head. "Never that." His eyes came back from beyond the circle of light. "And now it isn't? 'Written all over me,' I mean?"

"Now it isn't," Barker Caldwell said.

He didn't ask why, and Bill wasn't sure that he knew why. Not exactly, anyway. He supposed it was his people's eagerness to learn, their simple trust, their need.

God knew it had nothing to do with Jane and Paul Hamlin . . .

The cluster of cherries on Mrs. Gray's new black felt bobbed angrily.

"Well, if you ask *me*—"

"I don't rec'llect anybody askin'."

Mrs. Gray tossed her head. "You wouldn't, Melvina Mason! Anything Jane Langford does is all right with you—and I don't mind saying I'm surprised! Poor dear Brother Latham over there among those heathens and her forgetting to tell the police a thing like that! *Forgetting!*" Mrs. Gray let her arch gaze go around the church basement where the Ladies' Aid held its meetings. "I wonder."

"Lucy Gray, you take that back!"

"Why, Melvina? Would you have forgotten? The man was obviously a drug addict; Dr. Jane says so herself."

Granny's lips pressed tight. Dr. Jane had said no such thing, leastways not to Lucy Gray. To that policeman, maybe, and to Paul Hamlin, and for the life of her, Granny couldn't see how it had got out.

Granny opened her mouth, but the gavel was rapping smartly and she closed it again. Let Lucy Gray have the last word, she thought. She'd have it anyways, no matter what.

With a tiny, tremulous sigh, Granny smoothed the plum-colored crepe of her skirt where she had been pleating it between worried fingers. She didn't like the way the town was all stirred up, and even if Paul Hamlin was right and it'd all blow over, she wished the preacher was here.

'Course, she followed up the thought, it'd take more'n Bill Latham to make Lucy Gray hold her tongue. Look at the way she'd talked about the Delafield boy, and him president of the Student Council in the high school.

Why—

Granny caught her breath. That pain! Jabbing behind her breastbone that way, hadn't—had it for a—long time. The pills. Her fingers fumbled with the purse Sue had given her for Christmas, but liquid fire was running down her left arm now, and she couldn't breathe—

Sam Christy gave up trying to peer at the column of mercury and waited, as intent on Dr. Jane's face as if he, too, could hear the steady pulse that was drumming in her ears.

"What is it, Dr. Jane?" he asked anxiously when she had both the systolic and diastolic readings.

Jane began to unwind the sphygmomanometer's gray cloth sleeve. "Better than you've had for a long time, Mr. Christy." She told him the reading. "Pretty soon we'll have that down to one ninety over one ten and you'll be fit as a fiddle."

Well, almost as "fit," but she didn't tell him that.

"You and me'll lead the grand march at the spring festival."

"It's a date."

The old man's sigh was noisy. "If they have the spring festival," he said. "The way Halesville's tore up—"

Jane said, "I know," and nothing more. Sam Christy was one of those to whom she didn't have to explain anything.

He believed her, believed in her. But there were others—

She stood at the window for a brief, unhappy time after he had gone, looking out at the Old Doctor's rose garden and, across it, the big square old brick house where Dr. Ed lived—and was conscious of neither. Halesville was more than "tore up." Ron Delafield in jail, and she, Paul, and the dark, wild-eyed man on every tongue—Jane shuddered. She hadn't thought it could happen to her, but it had happened, it was happening.

Why couldn't she be like Paul? "Good Lord, Jane, it's not the end of the world!" he had burst out half angrily the other day. "You didn't expect some of the smear not to rub off, did you?"

Miserable, Jane turned from the window. She had patients waiting. She couldn't just stand there.

Besides, Paul was right. It would pass.

She went into the waiting room. "You're next, Mrs. Woods?"

"I guess I am."

Wheezing, Amelia Woods pushed herself up from the brown leather divan which Paul said had been ancient thirty years ago, and Jane thought worriedly, She's no better.

The telephone rang; she could hear Paul answering it. "Dr. Hamlin speaking." Then he was standing in her doorway.

"Jane. Jane, it's Mrs. Mason. She's had a heart attack at the church."

The church, the ambulance, the hospital telescoped in Jane's memory. She was a doctor, yes—she had seen heart attacks before. But this was different. This was Granny, and an angina brought on because of her.

She had gleaned enough of the talk around her to know that. Granny had defended her, and if Granny died now— Tears were hot in her throat and in her eyes as she bent to kiss the pale, cool forehead.

Granny didn't open her eyes, but the pathetically thin fingers tightened on Jane's. Jane patted them.

"You rest now, darling. Sue and I will be right here."

"No—need of that."

It was a whisper, so weak a whisper that the pale lips seemed barely to move.

"Don't try to talk, Granny," Sue pleaded. "And don't argue." From somewhere she summoned a cheery smile into her voice, although her face looked ready to crumble. "There are two of us, Granny darling!"

The long hours passed somehow. Seven o'clock. Ten. Midnight. Granny was restive, but her pulse seemed stronger. Rest, and no excitement, absolutely no worry— Dr. Jane bit her lip. No worry, when all of Halesville was on its ear.

"Would you and Miss Latham like a cup of coffee?" Miss Lancaster put her head in the door to ask.

"I would. Sue?"

"You go ahead, Jane." Sue glanced at Granny. "I—I'll have mine later."

Jane nodded and followed the nurse along the hall to the small kitchen from which food cooked in the huge kitchen downstairs was served out to the patients. The coffee was perking merrily on a hot plate.

"Heavenly aroma, isn't it?"

Miss Lancaster nodded. "There's nothing like it when it's one-ish."

Then it was two. And three.

And then dawn was tingeing the east, at first with only wisps of the coldest, palest gray, then with mother-of-pearl, and mauve and pink and then a sunburst of red-gold as the sun nosed above the horizon. Granny slept, restfully, restoratively, for the first time that night.

The next days were anxious ones. Granny Mason slept and rested, and listened to the news brought her by Dr. Jane, Sue, and the Old Doctor. Sue spent most of her time at the hospital when she wasn't chauffeuring the Old Doctor back and forth, and except for the afternoons when Paul was at the office in Stewart, Dr. Jane saw only the patients who were her "regulars."

Thank goodness there was Paul, she thought more than once as she hurried back to the hospital. What would she have done without him?

Through all this, not just Granny's illness—

More days. Granny was beginning to show improvement now, although Dr. O'Donnell still shook his head at Jane when they went into the corridor.

"She's better," he would say. "But very weak."

Or, "A valiant heart, that one."

Granny's was, Jane thought now, remembering Dr. O'Donnell's words. Valiant. And loyal—to her and to Bill Latham.

If only Granny would try to like Paul.

But Granny was Granny, and to her Paul was—Jane wasn't quite sure what. Sometimes she thought it was more than Bill, but it couldn't be.

It's just that Granny had her heart set on us marrying. What else could it be?

Paul had a perfect right to give up his practice in New York and come out here. After all, she had chosen country practice. Why shouldn't Paul? And why should Granny wonder out loud that he had?

"*If the practice was as good as he said it was.*" Granny had said that pointedly, and Dr. Ed had chuckled.

"Tut, tut, now, Melviny. A man's got a right to better himself, and I expect doctors are a dime a dozen in New York."

Remembering, Jane watched a splatter, and another, and another, on her windshield. It wasn't cold, thank goodness. It wouldn't be one of those January rains that chilled you to your marrow. She must remember to ask Paul about Mrs. Neidlinger's "j'ints," she thought. She hadn't been to Stewart for so long, and she missed it. Mrs. Neidlinger's "j'ints," and old Mr. Henry's "hay fever, consarn it!" Never just "hay fever."

By the time Jane reached Martinsburg, the pelting storm had subsided to a drizzle. Leaving her car in the physicians' parking area, she ran for the ambulance entrance.

Dr. Andrews was in Emergency, bandaging somebody's forehead—where it had banged against a windshield, Jane ventured a guess as she hurried past. The red light was on over X-ray, and in the next room Dr. Jancieski was dictating to his secretary.

"Dr. Fielding," the intercom began intoning, the girl's voice sounding hollow and unreal. "Dr. Fielding, please call your office. Dr. Fielding—"

"Good evening, Doctor," a group of students returning to the nurses' residence where they lived chorused, and Dr. Jane said pleasantly, "Good evening."

"Dr. Winters," the intercom began again. "Dr. Winters, call Extension Three O. Dr. Winters, call Extension Three O, please."

O. b., Jane thought, going through the foyer and along the first-floor corridor to Granny's room.

"Hello. It's raining."

Granny nodded. "I been watchin'."

"I brought your tatting."

Jane set the sewing basket on the bed and turned quickly to take off her coat. She didn't want to see Granny's thin, trembly hand go out to the basket, touch it lovingly, as if she had expected never to see it again.

"Where's Sue?"

"I sent her out. No sense in a girl like her bein' cooped up here. B'sides, I wanted the paper. You and Sue and Ed Johnson don't tell a body a thing." Lips pressed tight, she looked at Jane. "They ain't found hide ner hair of that man yet."

"No."

"And people's still gossipin' ther fool heads off, I reckon."

Impulsively Jane kissed her. "Granny, Granny."

"I thought they was." She lay quiet for only a moment. "When can I go home?"

"Now, Granny—"

"Like I told Ed Johnson yestiday, they's things that need doin'."

And undoing, Jane thought.

CHAPTER 14

The house was still. Jane didn't know what had wakened her. It wasn't the rain. Its gentle patter on the roof was a lulling sound, not a sound to set every nerve to tingling.

For the briefest instant she half-expected the telephone to ring again, but it hadn't been the telephone, either, she thought. When Clara Mae rang in the night it was as if to wake the dead.

There wasn't even a wind to rattle a shutter or sing its lonely song to the eaves.

She lay listening. The rain pitter-pattered, a quiet sound, as if the drops were walking on tip-toe across the steep-pitched roof. A rain to sleep by, not to waste lying wide-eyed, straining for a noise that probably hadn't been in the first place.

That was it. She hadn't heard a thing. Or perhaps it had been a car, or the Page's dog. She rose on one elbow, pummeled her pillow, lay down again.

If one of her patients complained of sleeping as fitfully as she had slept tonight, she'd—There! There it was again! A low, almost faint *creeeaakkk*.

As if somebody was trying to close that shrieky door without making any noise.

The thought leaped through her mind as she tumbled out of bed and grabbed up her robe. If she could get downstairs in time, turn on the outside light— But for heaven's sake, who would be prowling? In *there*? There was nothing but that mess of junk Bill hadn't gotten around to cleaning up.

She was downstairs, then, and in the kitchen punching the button that flooded the breezeway and the back yard with light.

No one.

No sign that anyone ha— The reassurance turned cold behind her breastbone. Unbelieving, she stared at the dampish splotches that could be only footprints *going straight to that door!*

Someone was in there! No—the old iron bolt that fastened the hasp was in place. But someone had been—

"What's the matter?" Sue whispered at her elbow.

"I thought I heard something." No need to alarm Sue. And Granny, who had come home yesterday.

She turned out the light before Sue could see the telltale prints. "Is Granny asleep?"

"Yes." And, "What did it sound like?"

"I don't think I'm sure," Jane fibbed. "Probably a dog nosing around. Or," she summoned a light laugh, "nothing at all. I'm jumpy tonight."

Certainly Sue could understand *that*.

But Sue was looking at her strangely. "I'm going to call Paul."

"For goodness' sake, what for?"

Sue didn't answer. Already she was giving the number to a sleepy Clara Mae Oley. Jane glanced at the clock. Not quite two. By morning those footprints would have dried and no one would have known.

Then Sue was hanging up, frowning. "He doesn't answer."

"Probably he's out on a call. I've an idea Clara Mae has been letting me take it easy."

Which wasn't the truth at all, and Sue knew it. It was just that people—some people, Jane thought unhappily and then didn't finish it.

"Where there's smoke there's fire," people were saying

knowingly if contritely, and she couldn't ignore the glances, the whispers, the conversations that ended with awkward abruptness when she approached or had subjects changed so fast that at least one of the conversationalists was left floundering. Paul said she should, but she couldn't. Biting her lip, she fled.

Morning came, finally, a belated graying of the darkness for, although the rain had stopped, the clouds still hung low and bulging and seeming scarcely to move. Jane hadn't slept.

Too much misery had plodded heavy-footed through her mind. Too many questions had probed and prodded and nagged—and refused to be answered.

Unable to lie still any longer, she rose.

She had to do something.

But what?

Thank goodness Granny was home and content. She could look after her, and the Old Doctor and Mrs. Dawson could run in. But no other visitors just yet. Not while the town was in such a furore.

Thinking that, Jane dressed in the brown suit and pumpkin-gold blouse without being aware that they were the brown suit and the pumpkin-gold blouse. If she could find where the talk was stemming from— It could be that way, she thought.

A word here. A sly insinuation there. Just enough to keep it going, while whoever killed Mr. Bates escaped unscathed?

It might not have been the frantic-eyed man at all. Lieutenant Jefferson could have been right; perhaps he was just someone who hadn't wanted to consult a woman doctor.

But if that were the case, why hadn't he asked where he could find Paul? Or gone to someone else?

For he hadn't. The police had checked every physician around and no one had treated him. Jane frowned. It didn't make sense. If the man had been as desperate as he had appeared to be—

"Hamlin!" He'd almost gasped Paul's name. "Where's Doc Hamlin?"

Jane could hear him yet. He had been—well, if not desperate—driven. He could have gone looking for Paul and, not finding him, decided to try the drugstore.

But why Paul?

"Hamlin! Where's Doc Hamlin?"

Don't be a bigger fool than you can help, Jane Langford! Of course he knew Paul's name!

A stranger, he had stopped to ask someone where he could find a doctor.

"Now you listen to me, Ed Johnson!" Granny Mason folded her arms across her thin chest. "You can set still and let be said the things that's bein' said if you want to. I ain't goin' to!"

"Tut, tut, Melviny."

The Old Doctor wagged his head admonishingly and peered at her over the gold-rimmed spectacles. "Janie's going to be all right."

" 'Course she is!" Granny snapped.

"Well, then," the Old Doctor took off his glasses and began polishing them, "let's concentrate on you. You oughtn't to get upset, you know that, Melviny."

Granny did know. Her heart was thumping along at a great rate. But somebody had to do somethin', although just what it should be Granny hadn't decided yet.

How could a body decide *anything*, she asked herself irritatedly, when she didn't know half what was goin' on? She almost wished that uppity Lucy Gray'd drop by. Then she bet she'd find out the lay of the land.

"I ain't upset half like I'm goin' to be if somebody don't tell me a few things. Dr. Jane and Sue, bless ther hearts, treat me like they sceert I'll break."

The Old Doctor polished his glasses to within an inch of their lives and with a sigh you could have heard upstairs put them on. Granny tatted on, waiting. Patiently, now. He was goin' to tell her. Put to him like that, she knowed he would—

"That's where I'm going to sow the clover," Larry said, pointing to the field across the lane.

Sue Latham nodded disinterestedly. She didn't see why Granny had to send her out to the farm this morning anyway. Larry could take care of himself; he was a good farmer and he knew where the clover should go this year.

"Ought to grow enough to feed through the winter," he went on. "Then in the spring I can sell those feeder steers—"

Which were part of the dream, too. Young steers gaunt from the Western ranges, fattened on pasture and hay and corn he grew himself. Sue's nod was absent, and he gave her a puzzled, hurt look.

"You're not listening."

"Yes, I am. But I was thinking, too."

"You're always thinking."

He didn't add "about Paul," but he might as well. It was there, in the sudden tautness that came into his voice, as if his throat hurt, in the way he looked away from her.

But this time he was wrong. Oh, she had been thinking about Paul all right, in a way. That he must have hated getting out in the rain last night, that it probably had been one of those impossible drives—he said they always were on bad nights. But mostly she had been thinking about that noise she'd heard, for all the world like someone walking around the house on that old brick walk. And then Jane slipping downstairs in the dark and trying so hard to fool her . . .

"Larry—"

She hadn't intended to tell him, but suddenly the words were pouring out. The footsteps she had heard, Jane pretending that she wasn't frightened—and this morning slipping out to that little building where Bill had been going to have his study . . .

"She was inside a long time, Larry," she finished, "and then she looked all around the house, outside. But you know how it is when it's been raining all night."

Larry nodded.

"Anyway, when I heard him, he was on the brick walk. He wouldn't have left tracks."

"What's out there?"

"That's the funny part. Nothing but junk. You know— old books, broken furniture, old medicine bottles, fruit jars, mice."

Larry's eyes roamed next summer's clover field and the woods beyond it while he thought it over.

"I don't like it," he said finally. "Not on top of everything else."

Sue stared at him.

"Don't you see, Sue? It doesn't add up to just prowling. Who would?" He shook his head. "No sir, it's tied to this other—all this—talk."

"You mean someone is trying to frighten Jane?" That seemed a little foolish. If it were that, he would have made more noise, she thought. Like throwing a brick through a window, or tossing a stink bomb. She'd read something like that in the papers the other day. "I—I don't think it's that, Larry."

"Well, it was an idea."

He picked up a clod, sent it whizzing to smack into smithereens against a fence post. "What does Doc Hamlin think about it?"

"I don't know. I tried to call him last night—this morning—but he was out on a call."

Another clod whammed the fence post.

"Just take a look at that, Dr. Jane!" Slowly, pathetically slowly, Joe Hiram closed his injured hand. "Slow motion but, Doc, I'm adoin' 'er!"

Jane said warmly, "I'm glad."

"No grip yet," Hiram admitted. "But know what Manning says?"

"No."

The big farmer grinned. "I ought to get down on my knees to you. You and Doc Laird, both."

Jane shook her head. "Not to us, Mr. Hiram. There are a lot of things doctors can't do—alone."

"Yeah. I know."

With a smile, Jane thrust out her hand. "Let's feel that grip."

"Put 'er there, Dr. Jane!"

It wasn't much of a grip, but it would be. Exercise, even handshaking, squeezing on a dimestore rubber ball— Feeling better than she had felt for days, Jane watched him go into Physical Therapy for another treatment.

She went along the corridor toward the lab. They should have that basal metabolism by now, she was thinking when the intercom began intoning:

"Dr. Langford, please call the switchboard. Dr. Langford—"

Jane hurried into the lab, where another loudspeaker was droning "—call the switchboard immediately. Dr. Langford—" She picked up a telephone, said, "This is Dr. Langford," into it.

"Just a moment, please."

Then a crisp, efficient voice was saying, "Surgery!"

"Dr. Langford," Jane told it.

"This is Miss Delman, Doctor. Dr. Winters wants you to scrub up at once. He is doing an emergency Caesarean, an accident victim—"

"I'll be right there, Miss Delman."

The basal metabolism would have to wait, but it could.

Paul would see the patients who might come; they would probably be relieved not to have to face her, anyway. Resolutely, Jane shoved *that* from her.

Dr. Winters needed her, *wanted* her to assist. Tom, at least, didn't think she—

She wouldn't think about that, either. Besides, Paul was probably right. She was self-conscious, imagining things. Of course Jace Perry had shot off his mouth at the Medical Society meeting the other night, but Fielding had shut him up quick—and she knew Jace.

That was the trouble, Jane thought now. She *did* know Jace.

Then the sterile, antiseptic- and anesthetic-smelling world that was Surgery enveloped her and Jace Perry didn't exist. Jane scrubbed up in a hurry, was helped into surgical gown, cap and mask by Nurse Delman.

They were operating immediately, on a girl no older than Sue, a tiny wisp of a thing eight months pregnant and dangerously hurt when her husband's car collided with another Behind her mask, Jane wet her lips. Could they save the baby—and the girl, too? She was such a child herself . . .

She wasn't thinking, then. At least not as Jane Langford. She was Tom Winters' second self, her skillful hands, her every thought attuned to his. Dr. Reynolds was there, and Miss Delman. And other nurses, and the anesthetist, the medical technologist who had done an emergency blood typing before they gave the transfusion.

"Blood pressure dropping!" The anesthetist's voice whipped through the room.

"Five hundred cc's Type A," Dr. Winters said, and a figure in white sped to the blood bank.

She was back in seconds and the blood was being transfused into a vein . . . Then the baby was delivered, and Jane and Dr. Reynolds took over while Dr. Winters worked with the baby.

He isn't crying— Jane was only half aware of the thought. And then he was, a thin, mewing wail, like an abandoned, frightened kitten, and Dr. Winters was saying sympathetically, "Go on, honey, squall. I don't blame you."

"Suture," Jane said. "What's the blood pressure now?"

The anesthetist told her.

Up. If they could keep it that way while they repaired the accident injuries . . . The baby was a girl, "spittin' image of her mother and yowling her red head off." Sometime during the next hours Jane heard someone say that. She didn't know who, it was just a voice, detached, strangely neither male nor female. Just words that come floating and are heard with the part of you that isn't immersed in the delicate task of tying off a vein or probing carefully, carefully . . .

Jane had lost all track of time. You do that when a life depends on you, and it doesn't matter whether you're the chief surgeon or the student doing your turn in Surgery. Every shred of your awareness is focused, not on the patient as a *patient*, but on your part in *this* fraction of an instant in making possible his recovery. You glance at a gauge and repeat its reading; at the precise instant he's going to need it you pass scalpel, retractor, hemostat to the surgeon. Perhaps you are the surgeon, dissecting, searching, repairing, or you're merely standing by. It doesn't matter. You're a part of the team. "Sweat," Jane said, and a nurse blotted the beads of perspiration from her forehead.

"Thank you."

Outside, the temperature might be plummeting, but she felt wringing wet. So, she knew, did Dr. Reynolds and Dr. Andrews, who had joined them. The great battery of lights, the tension . . . Were they succeeding? Or was the girl's life slipping away even as they fought to save it?

Tomorrow, next day, a week from now they might know . . . "Pulse?" Dr. Andrews asked.

And then, "Respiration?" . . . "Blood pressure?"

It was over, finally. Exhausted, Jane untied her breathing mask. They were wheeling the patient out now, to the recovery room where Miss Bailey would count every pulsebeat, almost. With a body as battered as that one, from the accident injuries, the Caesarean, and the shock of both, it was going to be that close, Jane knew.

"Good job, Jane."

"And yours."

Dr. Andrews smiled. "Thanks." Then, "You and Reynolds worked together before?"

Jane shook her head.

"I'd have sworn you had."

The operating room was a changed world now. Gone were the tensions, the urgency. Letdown. That was these minutes during which tired, taut bodies and minds relaxed all at once after the long strain, when one of the orderlies teased the surgical student, "Prettiest shade of green I ever saw!" When the pleasantest words in the world were "Good job" from

CALLING DOCTOR JANE

Dr. Andrews. Soap to his elbows, Dr. Reynolds came up. "Wish this was tomorrow."

Jane said, "I know."

"Wonder how her husband is?"

"D.O.A.," Dr. Andrews answered shortly, and Reynolds swore under his breath. Andrews went on, "I don't mean to snap. But it's a hell of a world, isn't it?"

Nobody disagreed.

The rain that had stopped with the dawn and threatened all day had begun again, a lazy, bone-chilling drizzle. Dr. Jane ordered another cup of coffee and sat watching the steam curl lazily up from it. She ought to call the office; she should have called the second she came out of surgery, but there had been that basal-metabolism report and a patient anxious for it.

And then she had realized that that odd swimming sensation was because she hadn't eaten, not even breakfast for which she'd had less than no appetite. She drew a deep breath. That wasn't like her.

"Hi, Jane. Andrews said he thought you were over here."

Dr. O'Donnell pulled out a chair, sat down opposite her. "I hear you've won yourself a laurel."

"I could use one."

The internist's eyes were steady on hers. "I've been hearing some of that. Not all of it, I daresay."

Not nearly all of it, Jane wanted to say.

He didn't wait for her to. "It's like that thing two, three months ago. It'll fizzle."

"This isn't fizzling."

"Baked ham on rye," O'Donnell told the waitress. "More coffee, Jane?"

"Thanks, no. This is my second."

"Coffee for me, then."

Jane drank the rest of her coffee and sat turning the thick mug in the ring it had left on the polished table top. She was running away, sitting here, she was postponing the inevitable . . .

"Jane—"

Dr. O'Donnell waited until the waitress had placed his coffee and ham on rye. Then, "I've been wanting to see you. And not wanting to." He studied the sandwich. "I'm still not sure which."

Again that pause, as if he *still* wasn't. He took the plunge, then, "What has Dr. Johnson got on his mind, Jane?"

"Dr. Ed?"

Which was inane, for of course he meant the Old Doctor. There wasn't any other Dr. Johnson around here.

O'Donnell nodded, said, "He swore me to secrecy. But he has been in twice for examinations. Says he's thinking of resuming practice and—"

CHAPTER 15

Jane drove home in a state of shock. Dr. Ed planning to resume practice and not telling her! *Not wanting her to know.*

She couldn't believe it, and yet it was true, it must be true! Why else would he have asked Dr. O'Donnell not to mention his visits?

But why had he?

Why, why, why?

The question beat at her, drumming through her brain until she thought she would go mad. Dr. Ed was on her side, he knew her, he trusted her. And yet—

Automatically, as she was doing everything else now, Jane signaled to the driver behind that she was slowing down when one of the semi-trailers bound for Clay Morton's factory toiled up the hill ahead of her. Then they were at the crest, the lights of the motel were twinkling through the dusk . . . and then the blacktop road that led from the highway into Halesville, glistening slickly where her headlights blazed a path through the rain.

The truck driver was cautious, and wary of that narrow bridge. He should be. The thought nudged through her worry, but only briefly. Dr. Ed mustn't resume full practice; his heart wouldn't let him.

Limited practice, perhaps. Dr. O'Donnell agreed that a limited practice, very limited, at least at first, might be the thing—might even be good for him.

But full time?

The internist had shaken his head. "I thought you might talk him out of it."

"When he hasn't asked me?"

Jane bit her lip. She could stand the rest of them, their distrust, their suspicion. Perhaps even in time she could live it down. But to have the Old Doctor doubt her—

The little white clapboard clinic was dark. Paul had gone —to his apartment or out on a call. With a puzzling sense of relief, she thought that. She didn't want to see anyone, not even Paul, just now.

And that was wrong. She had hidden long enough. If she didn't start to fight back now, it was going to be too late. Not quite sure where the surge of strength had come from, she sat in the car for minutes, analyzing it.

She was Jane Langford who had pulled herself up by sheer determination. She hadn't gotten her M. D. by not facing up to things. She wouldn't keep it that way.

Malpractice.

The word stabbed through her. She hadn't, but if the whispers persisted long enough . . . Even the operating room "laurel" Dr. O'Donnell said she had won today wouldn't mean a thing, then.

After a time, she got out and let herself into the darkened clinic. She didn't turn on lights; she didn't need them. She knew every inch of the offices, the tiny laboratory, the examining rooms.

"That you, Janie?"

Jane's heart turned over. Dr. Ed!

"Yes."

Dr. Ed, a short, not paunchy figure sunk meditatively in the old swivel chair, was almost lost in the darkness that seemed to have crept in out of the rain. The chair creaked a protest, as it always did, when he leaned forward to snap on the equally ancient gooseneck lamp.

"We've been worried about you, Janie."

"I'm sorry." She set her bag on the desk. "There was an accident, and emergency surgery." She told him about the operation. "Afterwards, of course, I had my patient to see and then I ran into Dr. O'Donnell."

A tiny silence before the Old Doctor heaved himself out of the chair.

"Better be calling the house, Janie. Melviny's a mite worried."

The rain stopped in the night, but the thawing temperatures had released frost in the ground and morning found

Halesville blanketed by fog. "Regular peasouper," Sue called it, and Jane agreed with her. The Old Doctor's big, square brick house across the street was barely visible, the trees behind it toward the river, and the clinic, were completely obliterated.

A morning for dented fenders and heads, Peter Farley would have said when they were manning the Emergency Room at City Hospital, Jane thought. Dented heads and broken bones . . . She put the coffee on while Sue got out the bacon and eggs.

"How many, Granny darling?" Sue sang out, and disappeared across the hall into Granny's bedroom to find out.

"Land sakes, child, one."

"One, sunny side up, coming up!" Sue danced back, bubbling despite the fog.

Jane leaned her forehead against the windowpane and watched the fog hang motionless in the elm tree. It was an enchanted world—or could be. Would it ever be again, for her?

The fear that it would not be stirred again. She put it down, as she had been putting it down for days and weeks now. The doubt, that plaguing, gnawing *what?* that was dodging about in her subconscious. She had almost had it then—

"I'm going to the office."

"Without breakfast?" Sue practically yelped.

"I'll put the pot on." All of a sudden she had to get away.

She was sitting at the Old Doctor's desk—her desk—when the telephone rang.

And rang again, peremptorily, banishing any thought she'd had about not answering it. "Dr. Langford speaking."

"What's the matter, darling?"

Paul!

"Nothing."

"It certainly didn't sound that way when Sue called. You had her worried." And after the briefest pause, "I'm coming right down."

He hung up before she could protest, and Jane thought, Darn Sue, anyway. I'd better call her.

But the line was busy. Paul, she thought. Reporting.

She hung up.

She shouldn't be angry with them, they both loved her, and at least this time Paul had been at home when they needed him. Or rather, when Sue thought she needed him.

Night before last he hadn't been—

She was measuring coffee into the percolator when he came. "Delighted to have you for breakfast, Dr. Hamlin."

He kissed her. "That's more like it."

"I'm sorry, Paul." She put the percolator on the hot plate, turned it on "high." "But all of a sudden I wanted to be by myself."

For a time he didn't say anything. Then, "So here I come barging in. Sorry."

"Oh, I'm all right now. Just don't blame me if I start thinking out loud."

Ever so gently he turned her to face him. "Maybe I can help. I want to, Jane. Believe me."

"I—I know."

He held her close, his jaw lean and cool and comforting against her cheek.

"Paul—"

"Yes, darling?"

She shook her head. What had she been going to say, anyway? Or had it been anything, except the sudden need to speak his name? She stepped out of the circle of his arms.

"I think our coffee is ready."

The factory whistle, ghostly, disembodied, muted by the fog, sounded while they were having second cups. Seven o'clock. Paul must have thought she had taken leave of her senses, dashing off to the office at such an hour.

No wonder Sue had called him. Jane sighed. It was being a difficult time for all of them.

"I've been thinking, Jane," Paul began after a longish silence. "If we—well, sort of reconstruct, it might help."

Jane shook her head. "I have, and it doesn't."

"With both of us reconstructing, it might. Start with Christmas Eve."

"You left early."

"And went straight home—"

They took it from there, first one, then the other fitting in a piece of the puzzle. The stranger whom nobody remembered seeing, or had seen since. Mr. Bates. Ronnie Delafield. The gossip that took on even more of a pattern now than ever . . .

"You see, darling? We're getting somewhere!"

But nowhere nearer knowing who had killed Mr. Bates, Jane thought, and that was the key.

"Ronnie Delafield wasn't prowling in Bill's den," she said, and Paul admitted that he hadn't been.

"I think you imagined that, Jane."

"The footprints, too?"

He shrugged them off. "Somebody cutting through."

"And vanishing into thin air at that door, I suppose?"

Paul laughed. "I guess I'm no detective." And after a moment, "Did you search the place thoroughly?"

She had looked. But *searched?* "Not very, I'm afraid."

"Then let's do that."

"Now?"

"Why not?" He grinned. "We might rustle some food, too."

Between the fog and the cobwebs, the summer kitchen was another world, a musty, dusty-smelling world of old books, newspapers, clothes, a chair with three legs, another with its stuffing spilling out, mute evidence of mice.

"You say Latham was going to make this his study?"

Jane nodded, and Paul, after another look around, said, "I'm afraid I don't see its possibilities. Looks like a good place to have nightmares. . . . Where do we start?"

They had had bacon and eggs, and Clara Mae Oley had been instructed to switch any office calls to the house.

"Anywhere, I suppose."

Paul eyed the stairway. "What's up there?"

"More of the same."

He groaned. "Well, I asked for it. You take that side, I'll take this." He kicked a dusty cardboard box whose contents went skittering and stooped to open it. "Marbles, for heaven's sake."

Marbles. A stack of *National Geographics*— Bill would love those! Then she remembered that Bill wouldn't be buying the house as they had planned. He'd be living in the parsonage again, he and Sue, with Mrs. Page coming twice a week to clean, the way she used to do.

Sue, she supposed, would be going to Africa for the next two years. Or back to Memphis.

"Telephone, Jane!" Sue called from the kitchen door.

Paul looked up from another box he was investigating. "I knew it! What's the weather report? In here you'd never know."

"Still foggy," Jane tossed over her shoulder.

Sue was waiting. "It's about Mrs. Woods."

Asthma, and this fog— "Yes?" Jane said into the kitchen extension.

"Mrs. Woods is bad, Dr. Jane." It was a neighbor calling.

"Have you given her the epinephrin?"

"Yes, but it doesn't seem to help." A note of panic had crept into the woman's voice.

"I'll be right there." She hung up, said to Sue, "Tell Paul, will you?"

She ran upstairs, unbuttoning the melon-pink coat dress, splotched now with dust, as she went. Swiftly she washed her hands, shrugged into the first thing she could grab and ran downstairs. Her bag was on the drum table, where it always was.

The fog seemed neither to have lifted nor fallen. There might not have been a sun; there wasn't even a pale blur to indicate that there was. And Boxtown seemed never to emerge from the dirty-gray, choking veils. On a morning like this, you'd think Clay Morton would let his fires go— you'd think, just once—

But the fog left no part of her for anger. Every shred of her alertness, every nerve strained to see. She was there, after an eternity. The smog nearly choking her, she ran inside.

"Dr. Jane! Thank the Lord you're here!"

The air in the house was a little better. A little, Jane thought. But the strangling gaseousness was there, or enough of it—

"Here's Dr. Jane, Mrs. Woods," the neighbor called, as they went into the bedroom.

Jane touched the wrinkled, convulsed cheek.

"I can't—breathe—I—can't even—stop cough—"

The paroxysm shook her entire body, rasping, wrenching, tearing at her throat and lungs.

"How long has she been like this?" Dr. Jane asked.

"The last hour. But she was wheezing bad before that."

Oxygen, Jane thought. Oxygen was what she needed. And there wasn't time for an ambulance to creep all the way from Martinsburg.

"Mrs. Woods," she said quietly, "I'm going to take you to the hospital for a couple of days."

The old woman nodded, gasping.

"The telephone?"

The neighbor pointed, and Jane telephoned first the state

police post at Martinsburg. It was an emergency, she told the officer who answered. Would they radio the car nearest to Halesville to meet her at the highway?

"Sure thing, Dr. Langford! You say you want an ambulance to come out from here meeting you? I'll call."

"Please do. Be sure they bring oxygen tank and mask."

"Right!"

Now to get Mrs. Woods' son at the factory— In minutes she was saying to Mrs. Woods, "Now, you just put your arms around my neck. That's it . . ." The neighbor woman followed with her medical bag.

It was a nervewracking drive, with a coughing, gasping woman in the back seat and the fog swirling in the ineffectual beams of her headlights. Was it beginning to lift, or was it only the car's painfully slow forward motion that made it seem to? Jane couldn't be sure. She couldn't be sure of anything but that she had to make it!

Granny fidgeted. Plague take it, the bed wasn't right. She thumped the pillow again, but that didn't help either. Paul Hamlin had no business out there prowlin' through the preacher's things. She didn't know what Dr. Jane meant, lettin' him.

Well, maybe they wasn't the preacher's, but he'd seen 'em first, she temporized. B'sides, what did Paul Hamlin think he was lookin' for anyhow?

He wouldn't know if anything was missin'. In that pile of trash, who would?

Granny lay frowning at the feathery swirls in the ceiling. He didn't think that sneak the other night might've hid somethin' in there, did he? Land sakes, who'd want to hide somethin' in Dr. Jane's summer kitchen?

'Course, nobody ever went in there, and it wasn't locked . . . Was that what Paul Hamlin was thinkin'?

That maybe he'd be comin' back— Granny made up her mind.

The room dipped a little bit, the way it did when she got up too quick, but by holdin' onto a chair— Dr. Jane would have a cat fit, Granny thought. But she had to talk to Ed Johnson and she didn't want Sue listenin'; the girl didn't have a brain in her head when it come to Paul Hamlin.

The hall, where the telephone was, seemed a long way, but she was there finally. She'd best wait just a minute, to catch her breath—didn't want Clara Mae Oley gettin' all excited—

"Git me Ed Johnson, Clara Mae."

"You're up, Granny! How nice!" Clara Mae rang the Old Doctor's number, then, and he was saying gruffly:

"Ed Johnson!"

"I want to see you, Ed Johnson."

"Melviny! What in tunket're you doing out of bed?"

"I'm out of it and I ain't right sure but what I'll stay out of it."

That'd fetch him ...

The fog was comin' down, it'd rain sure as God made little apples. Rainy now, and when Larry Burton needed rain for his crops, it'd be dry as bone dust, like as not.

She was steeling herself for the ordeal of getting back to bed when the brass knocker sounded. Land sakes, Ed Johnson must've run and he knowed better than to!

"Come—in."

Weak as a cat, she was, even her voice. She guessed she hadn't re'lized how sick she still was. Why, her heart was bustin' right out of her ribs!

"Yer not—I thought you was Ed Johnson."

The young man grinned. "Jim Hanna, ma'am. Doct—Heyyyy!"

They were lucky Dr. Hanna was there, the Old Doctor was saying. "If he hadn't been, I don't know, Janie." He shook his head.

Jane said, "I know." It frightened her, even now, to think about it.

She had come home from the Martinsburg hospital to find Granny sick as could be, with Paul, Dr. Ed and young Dr. Hanna in attendance, and a distraught and trying-not-to-show-it Sue hovering.

They still didn't know what had happened. Just that Granny had telephoned Dr. Ed. She wanted to see him and she had sounded—well, excited. Neither Sue nor Paul could imagine why.

Jane sighed.

There wouldn't have to be a reason. Hearts as bad as Granny's were like that. She could have been lying in bed and suddenly, from out of the blue, could have come that stabbing, twisting pain. She could have stumbled to the telephone and the Old Doctor could have mistaken fright for excitement ...

It was one of those lulls in afternoon office hours and Dr.

Ed and Dr. Hanna had come over. Dr. Hanna had finished his internship at City Hospital and was on the staff, but he had been thinking of striking out on his own. That was why he had gone to Florida on his vacation; he had thought he might establish a practice down there.

"But I don't know. Indiana's home," he said now. And went on thoughtfully, "A town like Halesville, not too far from Halesville—"

Sue, Jane thought and felt a stir of happiness.

The first in how long? Somebody said "Happiness was born a twin"—Byron, she thought. Bill would know . . .

Determinedly, she brought her attention back to now.

"If I had it to do over," Dr. Ed was saying, "I wouldn't have it any different. Country practice, boy. There's nothing—"

He broke off to answer the telephone at his elbow, "Dr. Johnson!"

Just as though he'd been doing it all these months— Jane couldn't help the pang that accompanied the thought.

The Old Doctor didn't wait to hang up. "One of Clay Morton's trucks has gone through that bridge! Janie—"

The truck had jackknifed as it went down, and the trailer had crumpled the cab like matchwood instead of metal. The driver was trapped; they could cut him out with acetylene torches if it wasn't for the gasoline that had spewed everywhere, but—

As she hurried out of the car, Jane heard somebody say that, a voice in the crowd that already was pressing close to the bank. Another voice yelled, "Watch it! The load's slippin'."

It was. The trailer tottered, swayed, miraculously steadied, but for how long?

"The driver'll drown!"

If the load slipped, pushing the cab a foot farther, he would. Or be crushed to death.

"Let us through, please!" Paul's voice cracked over their heads.

"Let Langford give him some dope, Doc!"

A hand on her arm tightened. Dr. Ed's. "Dr. Ed—"

"Steady, girl."

Then they were on the riverbank, the horribly twisted cab, the driver—that gasoline! The smell of it rose sickeningly.

A man came scrambling up the bank. "It's no use—one leg's pinned! He's unconscious, bleeding bad—"

"Paul," Jane said over her shoulder as she started down. They might not have to amputate but they could if they had to, to save a man's life.

Paul Hamlin didn't even hesitate.

"Not me, Jane. The guy's probably dead, anyway, and that truck's going to—"

CHAPTER 16

Jane didn't hear the rest of it. There wasn't time to hear, or to think, even. Not about Paul. Or herself. A hand reached out to steady her. She was in water up to her knees, dirty, swirly, gasoline-y water, and a voice was almost shouting in her ear:

"You'll have to work fast, Dr. Jane! The truck's making the water back up!"

"Sluice around it!"

Jim Hanna's voice, crisp, authoritative. "But careful—if that truck slips—"

If the truck slipped—

But Dr. Hanna had come. Paul hadn't. A curious stillness had settled over the crowd on the bank. They were there; with a part of her that strangely wasn't half in, half out of that cab, working in twisted, cramped positions she hadn't thought possible, Jane was aware of them. And of Dr. Ed scrambling down the bank, splashing through the water to them.

Neither she nor Dr. Hanna told him he shouldn't have come. They needed him too badly for that.

They needed a *dozen* pairs of hands, that other Jane Langford thought once. But there wasn't room for them. There wasn't even room for two pairs, hers and Jim Hanna's, as they fought desperately to stanch the blood.

"Dr. Ed, if you can get in here," Dr. Hanna said. "The subclavian artery—"

The water was to her thighs now and seeping into the truck cab, almost to the trapped, twisted leg she was trying to free. Why didn't they dig faster?

A siren. The ambulance they had summoned to stand by, or a police car?

"Jim," Jane said, and Dr. Hanna's hands were there, where she needed them, applying pressure on the femoral artery to cut off the supply of blood to the leg. They were going to have to amputate unless— "Jim—"

She looked up, but not at Dr. Hanna. The truck driver, young, husky, one leg gone at the knee— "Jim, if someone could get a crowbar under that—"

That was jagged, tortured metal, the instrument panel, the steering post, Jane wasn't sure what, it was so warped and wrapped and twisted.

"It could jar the whole works down."

"I—know."

Their eyes met, and in Jim Hanna's Jane saw reflected her own urgent need to save this man, all of him, if they could.

"Crowbar," he said over his shoulder, and Jane heard somebody's sharp intake of breath.

The Old Doctor's? Or the concerted gasp from the crowd on the bank? A mutter ran through the crowd, there was a shout, another, and another siren galloping up. The water was down! Jane realized that all of a sudden. The trickle had drained from the cab.

"Crowbar, Doc," a new voice said. "Show me where."

Lieutenant Jefferson. "You'd better get back, Dr. Jane. This thing's apt to—"

He didn't finish. There was no need, not when the hazel eyes had answered him *that* flatly. *I'm staying.*

They didn't talk, then. It was one of those moments that words spoil, when held breaths tip the balances. With Jane easing the torn, shredded flesh away from the gnawing metal and Dr. Hanna managing somehow to keep pressure on that femoral artery, Lieutenant Jefferson slipped the crowbar between two lips of the wreckage and pried.

Later, when she could think about it, Jane realized she had expected the huge truck to come capsizing down in that moment. But it didn't. A shudder seemed to run through it, but it held, and the crowbar got another, sturdier bite.

Thank God he's unconscious, Jane thought, and then knew that it hadn't been a *thought.* Not an unspoken one. For Lieutenant Jefferson said tersely, "Good Lord, yes!" and found a new grip for his 'bar.

With an angry, protesting shriek, it tore away from the raw, bitten flesh.

Not much. But a little.

Warily, for the big truck had given another jerking shudder, Lieutenant Jefferson moved in to the attack. It had to be easy . . . easy—and it couldn't be. Jane was on her knees now, straining to free the leg while the policeman reached over both her and Dr. Hanna to work. There was no other way.

"Get out, Janie," the Old Doctor said. "Let me."

"No."

The crowbar grazed her hand, found a new grip. She could move the leg! She *was* moving it, gently, gently—

He was free; *they could get him out!*

It was over. Jane still couldn't believe it. Not even when she looked in there and saw Jim Hanna, one eye glued to the microscope examining a throat culture taken from the Cleves baby. Jim liked lab work and if they couldn't afford a technologist—well, that couldn't be helped. One day perhaps they could, but until then, he and Jane and Dr. Ed—

Jane turned away. She wasn't ready to think of that yet. Paul was too close to her still. She had been wrong, but how could she have been so wrong?

She could have suspected, she supposed. She should have asked questions. Even before that terrible Christmas Eve, she should have doubted.

But she hadn't. Paul had but to kiss her, to touch her— Jane's face flamed at memories. She had been a fool! Of course, the frantic-eyed dark man had known Paul! He had been coming to the office in Stewart ever since that day she'd overheard Jace Perry: ". . . *you'll* see *him, all right."*

It went back so much further than that. The Old Doctor had known, and Jane knew too, now. It had been Paul who had refused to see the Jennings woman. Dr. Laird, Dr. Andrews, Tom Winters all had known and Dr. Laird had come to the Old Doctor.

"We decided to sit tight," Dr. Ed told her. "After all, a man can make a mistake and regret it. But after Charley Bates . . . I—I hated to do it, Janie, knowing what Hamlin meant to you—"

The Old Doctor had telephoned New York. From Martinsburg, not Halesville. He hadn't yet forgiven Clara Mae for not telling him about the emergency call she'd put through to Paul that night, from the motel out on the highway.

Anyway, he'd gone on to explain, Paul had left New York

a jump ahead of an indictment. "On a narcotics charge, Janie. They just missed proving it."

Here they *would* prove it. They already had.

Jane closed her eyes for just a moment. If only she could close her mind as easily! she thought. But would she ever be able to do that?

The police watching the office in Stewart, and Jace Perry's office in Martinsburg—it had been Perry who had brought Paul to Halesville, they knew now. They hadn't dared let them come to Halesville; there was too much danger in that. Jane or the Old Doctor might be hard to fool. Jane bit her lip at that. *She* hadn't been.

She hadn't even seen the truth when that poor, desperate creature burst into the office. They had taken him into custody when he had gone to the Stewart office on his regular "call," and he had told them plenty.

More than plenty. Sure, he'd killed the old man. He had to, didn't he, when Doc Hamlin wouldn't let him have the stuff?

"All right, Hamlin." Jane hadn't known Lieutenant Jefferson could be so cold-steel. With disgust, revulsion. Directed at Paul.

Paul had stared back at him belligerently, not denying, and Jane, sitting off to one side, had died, just a little.

"*If we reconstruct together—*"

Trying to find out what she knew, all the time chuckling to himself that she was so stupid.

Now it was Lieutenant Jefferson who did the reconstructing. "You knew who killed Mr. Bates, Hamlin, from the first. You covered up with lies, insinuations against the Delafield boy and Dr. Jane. It must have been easy for a man like you—you and Dr. Perry.

"Between you, you had things pretty well sewed up, didn't you?" The lieutenant didn't even bother to sneer. "But you, Hamlin, being so co-operative, helping check those drug supplies. Is that when you filched the stuff you hid in Dr. Jane's summer kitchen?"

Paul hadn't flicked an eyelash. He wasn't answering anything until his lawyer arrived, he'd already informed them . . .

"For you, Jane," Dr. Hanna said, although she hadn't heard the telephone ring.

Jane picked up her phone. "Dr. Langford."

"Dr. Langford," Clay Morton's voice boomed in her ear, "there's a young man in my office. Big, burly character. Says he's going to wrap his crutches around my neck if I don't do something about that confounded smoke of yours—"

"It isn't my smoke, Mr. Morton," Jane reminded him.

"The devil it isn't!" he retorted, but pleasantly. "I just thought you'd like to know I've decided to do it." The old gruffness came back into his voice. "Just say Clay Morton squares his debts. This one's for a danged good truck driver."

"Asey, what in tunket are you up to?"

Bill Latham reminded himself of the Old Doctor. "Tunket" was his word, but nobody but the Old Doctor could put quite as much into it.

You're homesick, Latham, the preacher thought then. A year in Africa and you're homesick.

A year. It hadn't seemed a year in some ways. In others, it had seemed a year many times over. When he thought of Halesville and all that had happened there. "Asey, you're as bad as Granny when the Aid's coming. Stop fluttering."

"Doct' Donaldson, he come."

"So what? Al's been here before when the plane wasn't all spit and polish."

Asey-for-short grinned. And went right on fussing with his housekeeping. Chuckling, Bill went outside. May, he thought. The spirea would be blooming, the forsythia around the church already bloomed and gone in a shower of gold.

He'd bet Granny was about to bust a gusset over the new carpet. Granny had finally put it over. Not that it would make hearts any closer to God, he thought, but a new carpet was nice. Smoke-gray, Granny had written, with "little bitty" wine and black medallions in it. A good, utilitarian carpet that would last for another twenty-five years.

Off across the compound Keaa was hanging out her washing. Bright-colored pagnes, Asey's shirts and trousers. Bill smiled. He guessed Asey was reformed for sure now. Keaa would see to that.

It had been quite a wedding. Feasting, singing, dancing, shivareeing . . . Remembering, Bill went back inside. He'd better get lined up on Sunday's sermon. He'd planned to work on it tonight, but with Al coming— It wasn't Al's regularly scheduled visit and he hadn't sent word, but Asey said he was coming, so he was coming. Bill Latham had developed a healthy respect for his factotum's mysterious modes of communication. What Samuel Morse couldn't have done with Asey-for-short!

And a few jungle drums and native runners, Bill thought. He opened the Book. "Let us hold fast the profession of our faith without wavering—"

A good text. Good for Asey . . . good for Bill Latham. He leaned back, thinking about it.

"Hi, Bill!"

Before he knew it was time, Al Donaldson was there. A jubilant Al, who must have discovered a cure for encephalitis at the very least.

"Well, hello. Early, aren't you?"

"You're the one who was early. By about twenty centuries, judging from the look of you when I came in." Al grinned. "Where were you, man? Capernaum?" And without a pause, "Cablegram for you."

Bill opened it. " 'Arrive Kampala seventeenth—' Hey! That was day before—no, the day before that! Now *wait* a minute, Al! You're—she's—"

"Bill."

The voice was soft, scarcely more than a whisper, right behind him. "Bill, darling—" And somehow, she was in his arms, his lips were on hers.

Oh, Bill, Bill!

Darling, I almost was an awful fool!

SPECIAL OFFER If you enjoyed this book—and would like to have a list of other fine Bantam titles available in inexpensive paper-bound editions—you can receive a copy of our latest catalog by sending your name and address to CATALOG DEPARTMENT, BANTAM BOOKS, INC., 414 EAST GOLF ROAD, DES PLAINES, ILLINOIS.

ABOUT THE AUTHOR

ADELINE MCELFRESH has been a newspaperwoman for twenty years. She has served on various newspapers as feature writer, editor of the women's section and correspondent.

Miss McElfresh has always been interested in medicine. She has her own medical library, where she diligently researches material for her novels.

Adeline McElfresh has written twenty-six nurse and doctor stories, including the Dr. Jane series, which comes closest to her heart. Indeed, Miss McElfresh admits that she has always secretly admired and envied the character and career of her creation, Dr. Jane.

Her other interests include early Indian civilizations (especially the Maya), pioneer Americana and the Civil War (she's a dedicated Rebel).

Miss McElfresh lives in a rambly, nineteenth-century house in Vincennes, Indiana with her father and her kennel of thirteen dogs.

Millions of readers have enjoyed the rare mixture of sound medical understanding, poignant insight and scalpel-sharp portraits of women doctors and nurses in the novels of ADELINE McELFRESH. Have you read:

- Dr. Jane
- Dr. Jane's Mission
- Dr. Jane Comes Home
- Dr. Jane's Choice
- Calling Dr. Jane
- Dr. Jane, Interne

45¢ each

Buy these Bantam books wherever paperbacks are sold

Introducing
9 Bantam Gothic Novels

Haunted houses, sinister plots, dread forces of evil, mysterious deaths, obsessive love and revenge. All this and more in Bantam's new Gothic Novel Series. Written by some of the world's foremost Gothic writers, here are nine spellbinding tales not to be missed.

- [ ] **Jassy** Norah Lofts.................60¢
- [ ] **The Uninvited** Dorothy Macardle...60¢
- [ ] **The Web of Days** Edna Lee......60¢
- [ ] **The Fortune Hunters** Joan Aiken..60¢
- [ ] **The Unforeseen** Dorothy Macardle.60¢
- [ ] **Blue Fire** Phyllis Whitney..........60¢
- [ ] **The Queen Bee** Edna Lee.........60¢
- [ ] **Claire** Dorothea Malm..............60¢
- [ ] **The Return of Jennifer**
      Helen Upshaw...60¢

BUY THESE BANTAM BOOKS
WHEREVER PAPERBACKS ARE SOLD
OR WRITE:

BANTAM BOOKS, INC., Dept. GN, 414 East Golf Road, Des Plaines, Ill.
Please mail me the Bantam Gothic Novels checked above. I am enclosing $_____ (Check or money order—no currency, no C.O.D.'s please. If less than 5 books, add 10¢ per book for postage and handling.)

Name_____

Address_____

City_____State_____Zip_____

Allow 2 to 3 weeks for delivery

TEAR OUT THIS PAGE AND USE AS YOUR ORDER BLANK

Millions of copies sold at top prices! Now read them for just pennies!

BANTAM BEST SELLERS

Here is O'Hara's latest story collection, Hemingway's outstanding last work, and John Gunther's latest novel. Look over the list and order the ones you missed, at just a fraction of the price paid by millions for the same bestsellers in hardcover editions. Bantam's popular paperbacks are available at newsstands everywhere, or mail this page with check or money order directly to the publisher.

☐ **THE HORSE KNOWS THE WAY.** John O'Hara's newest collection of sizzling and superbly written stories. N3103 • 95¢

☐ **A MOVEABLE FEAST.** The famous Nobel Prize-winning author's own story of his wild, young years in Paris. N3048 • 95¢

☐ **THE LOST CITY.** John Gunther's exciting new novel about Vienna prior to the Nazi invasion. N2997 • 95¢

☐ **THE ITALIANS.** Luigi Barzini's wise and witty portrait of his countrymen's manners and morals. N3090 • 95¢

☐ **ONLY YOU, DICK DARING!** Merle Miller and Evan Rhodes' hilarious and true story that rocked the TV industry. S3045 • 75¢

☐ **BOYS AND GIRLS TOGETHER.** William Goldman's current controversial novel of five young people who come to New York to fulfill their dreams. N2981 • 95¢

☐ **THE SKI BUM.** Romain Gary's sensational novel of two youngsters whose affair is threatened by love and the world around them. S3114 • 75¢

☐ **JOY IN THE MORNING.** Betty Smith's heartwarming bestseller, the story of a young couple that marry against their parents' wishes. S2808 • 75¢

BANTAM BOOKS, INC., Dept. GA1, 414 East Golf Road, Des Plaines, Ill. Please mail me the Bantam Best-sellers checked above. I am enclosing $_____ (Check or money order—no currency, no C.O.D.'s please. If less than 5 books, add 10¢ per book for postage and handling.)

Name_____

Address_____

City_____State_____Zone____

Allow 2 to 3 Weeks for Delivery